FROM THE
NANCY DREW FILES

THE CASE: Editor Maxine Treitler is dead, and Nancy knows only one thing for sure: The butler didn't do it.

CONTACT: The late Dorothea Burden wrote the book on murder . . . now Nancy must read between the lines to find a killer.

SUSPECTS: Erika Olsen—*an editor from a rival publisher, she claims that Maxine stole the rights to Dorothea's last unpublished novel from her.*

Bill Denton—*Dorothea's former agent, he wants a cut of the novel's future profits, but Maxine promised to cut him off.*

Kate Jefferson—*tetary of the estate, she's he police . . . pert of her boyfrie*

COMPLI problem finding suspending someone who isn't; she'll hork her way through every twist and turn in the mansion to write a final chapter to this mystery.

D1018730

Books in The Nancy Drew Files® Series

Available from ARCHWAY Paperbacks

The Nancy Drew Files™

Case 76
The Perfect Plot

Carolyn Keene

AN ARCHWAY PAPERBACK
Published by POCKET BOOKS
New York London Toronto Sydney Tokyo Singapore

AN ARCHWAY PAPERBACK *Original*

An Archway Paperback published by
POCKET BOOKS, a division of Simon & Schuster Inc.
1230 Avenue of the Americas, New York, NY 10020

Copyright © 1992 by Simon & Schuster Inc.
Produced by Mega-Books of New York, Inc.

ISBN: 0-671-73080-0

First Archway Paperback printing October 1992

10 9 8 7 6 5 4 3 2 1

Cover art by Tricia Zimic

Printed in the U.S.A.

IL 6+

The Perfect Plot

Chapter

One

"HELP!" George Fayne exclaimed. "I'm being attacked by a road map!"

Nancy Drew laughed and brought her blue Mustang to a halt on the shoulder of a narrow country road.

She tucked a strand of reddish blond hair back behind one ear and glanced over at her friend. George's short, curly, brown hair was tousled and poked up over the road map that lay plastered to her body and face. "Maybe we should roll the windows up," Nancy suggested.

"And miss all this wonderful fall air?" George protested, peeling the map off herself. Her brown eyes sparkled as she took in the colorful foliage on either side of the road. "No way! Anyway, we

1

must be nearly at Mystery Mansion—unless I've gotten us completely lost."

Nancy pulled out an envelope and checked a page of directions. "No, this is right. We follow Farm Road Eight-Nineteen to the crossroads, then go left for two miles to the gates of the estate."

While George tried to figure out how to fold the road map back to a manageable size, Nancy turned on her blinker and put the car in gear. She was about to pull out onto the road when a horn blared from behind. A low, silver sports car roared past at high speed, missing them by inches. Nancy glimpsed the man at the wheel long enough to register his dark mustache and the pipe clenched in his teeth.

"What a menace," George said, shaking her head in disgust.

Nancy nodded. "I'm glad he's ahead of us now and not behind us." She checked the side mirror carefully before pulling onto the road. A few minutes later she spotted a sign.

MYSTERY MANSION
Museum & Conference Center

Underneath the words was the hand of a skeleton pointing to the left.

George grinned at Nancy. "I'm totally psyched. I mean, Dorothea Burden was my absolute favorite mystery writer. I can't believe we're actually going to a mystery conference at her mansion! Not to mention the fact that we'll get to rub elbows with mystery experts from around the country."

"I can't wait to see the exhibits," Nancy said, turning onto the side road. "They say Dorothea spent a fortune building Mystery Mansion. It's filled with rare books and an awesome collection of paraphernalia related to mysteries and real-life crimes."

"She could afford to spend a fortune," George commented. "Her mysteries were all best-sellers. It's hard to believe she won't ever write another one."

Nancy nodded her agreement. Even though she preferred dealing with real mysteries to reading them, she had been sad to learn of the mystery author's death the previous spring. "Still, it's great that she left her house and collection as a museum and library devoted to mysteries and crime detection," she said. "And to think that we've been invited for the first official function."

Nancy's invitation to the conference was the result of her growing fame as a detective. When she had called the Burden Foundation's secretary to accept, Nancy had managed to get invitations for her friends George Fayne and Bess Marvin, too. Unfortunately, Bess hadn't been able to come because of a cousin's wedding. George, though, had jumped at the chance. "I have a tennis match coming up," she'd said, "but I'll just bring my rackets with me since Mystery Mansion has a court."

"This must be it," George announced.

Nancy slowed down and looked to the right. A stone wall, topped with shards of broken glass set in cement, now bordered the road. Up ahead was the entrance with tall stone pillars flanking it on either side. On top of each pillar sat a brooding, winged monster, its chin resting on clawed hands. A bronze sign on one of the pillars proclaimed that this was Mystery Mansion, but the spike-topped iron gates were shut.

Pulling her Mustang close to an intercom box, Nancy pressed the button at the bottom. A tinny voice said, "Mystery Mansion—may I help you?"

"Hi, it's Nancy Drew and George Fayne," Nancy replied. "We're here for the conference."

"Okay. It's straight ahead," the voice said. There was a loud buzz, and the gates were swung back to allow them to enter.

As they followed the drive around a little clump of trees, George suddenly let out a low whistle. "Check it out!" she exclaimed.

An enormous stone mansion had just come into view. Nancy counted three floors of tall windows, as well as a row of dormers set into the gray slate roof. At the far end of the mansion, a circular tower rose two more stories, ending in a cone-shaped roof. Apparently the east wing, which the tower was attached to, was under repair. Scaffolding covered it almost to the top.

"It's pretty impressive," Nancy agreed. She followed the drive around a circular fountain filled only with dead leaves to a flight of wide stone steps leading up to the main doorway. As she pulled to a halt at the foot of the steps, the dark wooden door swung open.

Nancy half-expected to see an ancient and sinister-looking butler. Instead, a tall guy in his early twenties came out. His dark hair gleamed in the sunlight, and his polo shirt matched the blue of his eyes. As he came down the steps toward them, he smiled, and two incredibly cute dimples appeared in his cheeks.

"Talk about gorgeous!" George said under her breath.

"Hi," the young man said, bending to look in the passenger door. "I just buzzed you in, so I know you must be Nancy and George. But which is which?"

He gave each girl a warm smile as they introduced themselves. "I'm Patrick Burden. Let me give you a hand with your bags, then I'll show you where to put the car."

George handed him the two nylon bags from the backseat. "Patrick Burden— Are you—"

"Dorothea was my aunt," he explained. "She and Uncle Harrison helped bring me up after my parents died. I've always thought of this place as home, so I've stayed on to help sort things out and get the museum off and running. Hang on a sec—I'll just set your bags inside the door."

A moment later he returned, and George opened her door so he could climb into the backseat. Nancy didn't miss the smile he gave George before instructing, "Go to the corner of the house and turn right. The old stable yard is just at the back."

Nancy followed his directions and parked at the end of a row of half a dozen cars. As she was getting out, she noticed that the silver sports car that had almost sideswiped them earlier was parked two cars down.

"We're expecting a good crowd this weekend," Patrick commented after he and George got out on the passenger side. "But most people will have to stay at a hotel in town. We only have room for ten or so people here so far. We've got a lot of work left to do on the house."

Nancy and George followed Patrick past some construction equipment and a rose garden that needed tending to a set of french doors at the back of the house. Inside, they found themselves in a narrow room with floor-to-ceiling windows along one long side. White wicker furniture with bright yellow cushions was scattered throughout.

The late-afternoon sun was just beginning to fade, and a chill had crept into the room.

"This is the sun room," Patrick announced.

Nancy noticed a woman with shoulder-length gray hair and glasses sitting in one of the wicker chairs. She was reading from a pile of papers. As she finished a page, she'd drop it onto an untidy pile on the floor.

"That's Maxine Treitler," said Patrick. "She was my aunt's editor for years and one of her best friends. Aunt Dotty always said that Maxine deserved most of the credit for her success."

At the sound of their voices, Maxine took off her glasses and glanced up at Nancy, George, and Patrick. From the way she was squinting, Nancy guessed that the editor's eyesight wasn't very good.

"I'm so glad to meet you," Maxine said when Patrick introduced Nancy and George. "It's a pleasure to know young people who are interested in Dorothea's work."

"I've been a fan of hers for years," George said.

Maxine gave George a pleased smile. "You must tell me which of her books are your favorites. I must know every one of them by heart."

Before George could reply, Patrick cut in. "Maybe you two can talk later. George and Nancy just arrived, and I want to find Kate and ask her to show them to their room."

"Of course," Maxine said graciously. "It's

getting a bit chilly in here, anyway. I think I'll move inside." She felt around in her lap, found her glasses, and began picking up the manuscript pages from the floor.

"Who's Kate?" Nancy asked Patrick as they walked toward a wide doorway edged with beaded curtains.

"Kate Jefferson, the executive secretary of the Burden Foundation," he replied. "She used to be my aunt's secretary and companion. She really runs this whole show. Mystery Mansion would fall apart without her."

He led Nancy and George down a hallway and into a square entrance hall that stretched up more than three floors to a stained-glass skylight in the roof. The broad front door was directly in front of them. Sets of double doors led off to other parts of the house. At one side of the hall, a wide flight of carpeted stairs with a carved wooden banister led upward.

Patrick smiled at the awe on George's and Nancy's faces. "My aunt really liked the spectacular. That's probably one reason her books are so popular."

He had just retrieved the girls' bags from beside the front door when Nancy heard raised voices from an adjoining room. Two people came through a doorway to the right, talking heatedly. One was a woman in her midtwenties with a long oval face, dark eyebrows, and a black ponytail.

The severe effect of her ankle-length black skirt and scoop-neck black silk blouse was lightened a little by an antique gold necklace she wore.

Nancy frowned when she saw the woman's companion. It was the guy with the dark mustache who had sped past the Mustang earlier. He was wearing black corduroy slacks and a white fisherman's knit sweater.

"My job's a lot harder now," the man said, gesturing with his pipe. "With Dorothea gone, it's more difficult to sell the rights to her existing books. I can't use the possibility of a new book as a lure. I deserve to be compensated for the extra work."

"I'll take it up with Armand, first chance I get," the young woman replied wearily. "But I can tell you what he'll say. If ten percent was enough before, it should be enough now."

She glanced around. "Oh, hello, Patrick," she said, turning her back on the man. "I'm Kate Jefferson." She held out a hand to Nancy and George.

Patrick introduced the girls, then said to Kate, "I thought you might show them where they're staying."

Just then the man with the mustache strolled over to them. "Bill Denton," he said, nodding a greeting.

"We almost met a little while ago," Nancy said coolly. "We had pulled off to the side of the road, and you zipped past us at about seventy-five miles an hour."

"That's Bill," Patrick put in lightly. "Always in a hurry, even when he doesn't have any good reason to get where he's going."

"My get-up-and-go did a lot of good for your aunt, Patrick, and don't you forget it," Bill said emphatically. *"She* didn't forget—except when she was making her will."

"That's a discussion we can leave for later, Bill," Kate said smoothly. "In the meantime, I'm sure George and Nancy want to freshen up after their trip."

"That would be nice," George said. She took her bag from Patrick and slung it over her shoulder. Nancy did the same. Leaving Patrick and Bill Denton in the foyer, they started up the stairs with Kate.

"We've put you and most of the other guests on the second floor. I think you'll be comfortable," Kate told them.

As they walked down a long second-floor hallway, Nancy asked Kate, "Who is that man we were just talking to?"

"Bill? He was Dorothea's literary agent." Kate produced a large, old-fashioned brass key and unlocked a door on the left side of the hallway. "Here we are. You're in the Baker Street room."

"Isn't that where Sherlock Holmes lived?" asked George.

Kate nodded. "Exactly. Dorothea liked to give her guest rooms the flavor of different classic mystery stories. We have Honolulu in the 1920s, an English vicarage, the Maltese Falcon room . . . there's even one done up like a room in Paris a hundred fifty years ago. It's called the Rue Morgue."

George shuddered. "What a creepy name!"

"It's in honor of the classic story by Edgar Allan Poe," Kate explained. She pushed the door to the Baker Street room open.

Nancy's first impression was that the room was jammed with furniture. It wasn't really, but the floral wallpaper, heavy velvet curtains, and patterned brocade covers on the two beds seemed to fill up a lot of space. Two lamps with stained-glass shades cast mysterious pools of light on the oriental carpet. On the wall near the door was the framed cover of an issue of *Strand* magazine, in which the Sherlock Holmes stories had first appeared. A curved meerschaum pipe and a magnifying glass had the place of honor on the marble fireplace mantel.

"Wow," George said, dropping her bag on one of the beds. "This is amazing."

Smiling, Kate said, "Well, I have to get back to my duties. I can't believe how many details are involved in putting on a conference like this. Please come downstairs and meet the others when you're ready. We'll be in the living room."

"Thanks," Nancy said.

Once Kate was gone, George opened her bag and shook the wrinkles out of a sweater dress. "I think I'm going to like it here," she said.

Raising an eyebrow, Nancy said, "I know Patrick Burden likes having you here."

A slight blush rose to George's cheeks. "He *is* cute, but I'm not interested in dating a guy who doesn't live in River Heights."

George had recently ended a relationship with sportscaster Kevin Davis because it was hard for them to spend much time together. Nancy could understand why George wanted to avoid that situation again.

Crossing to the window, Nancy pulled back the curtains. Their room faced the front of the house. On the far side of the lawn by the wing under repair was a lacy white summerhouse surrounded by flower beds.

"Nan!"

At the strangled cry, Nancy spun around. The closet door stood open. George's jacket and sweater dress lay in an untidy heap on the floor. They were the only signs of her, though.

George had vanished!

Chapter

Two

NANCY RUSHED OVER to the closet. The interior was spacious, about four feet wide by six feet deep, with shelves and a clothes rod along the right-hand side. She didn't see anyplace someone could hide.

"George!" Nancy called, trying not to panic.

"Mmmpf." The faint sound was followed by a tapping noise that seemed to be coming from *behind* the left-hand wall.

Studying the wall, Nancy saw that it was paneled with cedar boards. A row of brass coat hooks were set into the paneling. Around one of the hooks, a semicircular mark was gouged into the wood, as if the hook had scraped against the wall while being turned.

"Hmm," Nancy murmured to herself. Grabbing the coat hook, she twisted it. It resisted for a moment, but then there was a small click. A section of wall moved inward.

"Nancy! Thank goodness!" George exclaimed, rushing out of the darkness and grabbing her friend's arm. Her face was pale, and there was terror in her eyes. "I thought I was going to be stuck in there for good!"

"What happened?" Nancy asked.

"Let me get out of here first," George said. She hurried past Nancy to sit on one of the beds. "That secret panel closes by itself. That's how I got trapped."

Nancy released the coat hook, and sure enough, the panel instantly swung closed.

"I started to hang up my jacket," George went on breathlessly. "I *would* have to pick that hook. Anyway, the wall suddenly moved back. I took a step forward to check it out without even thinking. Before I knew it, the panel closed again, and I was trapped in the dark. I felt around for a way to open the panel from that side, but I couldn't find anything."

She paused to sneeze. "I don't think anyone's dusted back there since this place was built."

"Secret panels, hidden passages—it's like something from a book," Nancy mused.

George stared at her. "It *is* from a book!" she declared. "One of Dorothea Burden's books! I don't remember the name of it, but a scene from it really stuck in my mind. This girl is chased through a maze of secret passages by a madman. Just when she thinks she's safe, her flashlight goes out."

"Hey, look," Nancy said, pointing. A flashlight rested on one of the closet shelves.

"I bet someone put it there on purpose," George said. Flopping back on her bed, she reached over and picked up a printed sheet from the bedside table. "Here's a schedule for the conference," she said.

Nancy began to take clothes out of her bag and put them in the dresser. "I practically have the whole thing memorized from the material they sent—mystery competitions, a mystery masquerade party, a tour of Dorothea Burden's collection of mystery paraphernalia—"

"Not to mention a talk given by famed teen detective Nancy Drew," George added, grinning at Nancy.

Nancy felt her cheeks grow hot. "After witnessing your disappearance just now, I bet this weekend is going to be mysterious in ways we never thought of!"

"Aunt Dotty loved to build things into this house that were mentioned in her books," Patrick told Nancy and George half an hour later. The girls had run into him on the stairs, where

George told him about the hidden door in the closet. "The secret compartment in the Baker Street room is just one example. I don't think any single person knows all the secrets of this house. My aunt probably didn't remember all of them herself."

Downstairs, Patrick led the girls across the entrance hall and through a set of doors to the wood-paneled living room. It was furnished with oversized, comfortable sofas and chairs. On the far side of the room, half a dozen people were clustered near an enormous carved-stone fireplace next to a second set of double doors. A cheery blaze crackled on the grate, filling the air with the scent of burning firewood.

Once Nancy, George, and Patrick had joined the group, Kate Jefferson introduced everyone. Nancy had already met Maxine Treitler and Bill Denton, so she made a special effort to remember who the others were.

A bald, portly, middle-aged man in a tweed suit turned out to be Professor Marsden Coining, a leading expert on popular crime fiction. He was chatting with an attractive young woman with pixie-cut blond hair, who was wearing a blue suit with a brightly colored silk square knotted loosely at her neck. Kate introduced her as Erika Olsen, a new senior editor at the publishing house of Cameron & Sweazy.

16

"Oh, Patrick," Erika said, taking his arm. "There's something I wanted to ask you." Glaring at Nancy and George, she walked him out of earshot.

George bent close to Nancy and whispered, "Look's like I've got competition—and I'm not even competing!"

Next, Kate introduced the girls to Julian Romarain.

"Hi, all." Julian appeared to be in his late twenties, with dark hair and a well-trimmed beard. He was wearing faded designer jeans, a tooled belt with a silver buckle, and a polo shirt with a little skull and the words *Murder to Go* embroidered on it.

"What's Murder to Go?" George wanted to know.

"That's my company," Julian replied. "We stage mystery weekends at romantic resorts. The guests try to solve mock crimes. We bring in experts, too. You know—detectives, mystery writers. It's a lot of fun."

"It certainly is," the woman next to Julian said. She was tall and slim with light brown hair. She had an ageless face—Nancy couldn't tell whether she was closer to thirty-five or fifty. "I've taken part in two or three of Julian's weekends, so I know."

"Thanks, Vanessa," Julian murmured.

George's eyes widened. "You're not Vanessa Van Ness, the novelist, are you?" she asked breathlessly.

The woman smiled. "Why, yes. Why do you sound so surprised?"

Nancy noticed George start to blush. "I love your books, but somehow I expected you to be—different."

Vanessa Van Ness raised one eyebrow. "You mean short and tubby, with white hair, a black dress, and a shawl around my shoulders?"

"Don't forget the high black shoes that button up the side," Professor Coining said.

"And the bag of knitting to hide a revolver in," Erika added as she and Patrick rejoined the group.

"No, no—the bottle of poison," Julian put in. "Revolvers are much too noisy and make a mess."

George's face had turned bright red, Nancy saw. She looked as if she wished she could sink right through the floor.

"Never mind, dear," Vanessa said, putting an arm around George's shoulders. "We're just teasing you a little. People so often expect me to be like the characters in my books. But as you can see, I'm not."

Turning to Kate, Vanessa asked, "When are we finally going to see the famous figurines?"

The change of subject was so abrupt that Nancy was sure Vanessa had done it to spare George any further embarrassment.

"We've been keeping them in the safe while we've had a special display case made for them," Kate replied. "But I'm glad to say the case is finished at last. We'll have a formal installation right after dinner."

Nancy remembered reading about the figurines in the conference pamphlet. "You're talking about the jeweled gold figures of the characters from Dorothea's novels, right?" she said.

Kate nodded. "Her publisher had them made for her, as a sign of appreciation for her wonderful books."

"Her very profitable books," Bill added.

"I can't wait to see them," Erika said excitedly. "They're legend in the publishing world."

While the others continued talking about the jeweled figures, Patrick said to George, "I hope you're enjoying yourself so far."

George returned his broad, warm smile. "We're having a terrific time."

"A lot of Aunt Dotty's collection is across the hall, in what used to be another sitting room," he continued. "How would you like a private tour later?"

"I'd love that," George replied. "I mean, *we'd* love it," she added quickly, glancing at Nancy.

Nancy was starting to feel like a fifth wheel. Saying she wanted to get some punch, she left George and Patrick.

She noticed that Vanessa was gazing at a painting of a man with a white beard. Nancy looked at the painting and was surprised by the way the man's eyes seemed to bore directly into hers. "Do you know who that is?" she asked Vanessa.

"Sure. That's Harrison Polk."

Nancy's face must have reflected the confusion she felt.

"Dorothea's late husband," Vanessa explained. "She used her maiden name for her books, you know."

"I didn't even know until today that Dorothea had been married," Nancy admitted.

Vanessa nodded sadly. "It was a great shock to Dorothea when Harrison died," she said. "He seemed to be in such splendid condition. He was still running marathons at the age of fifty-four. But one day a couple of years ago, he came in from playing tennis, stepped into the shower, and fell dead of a massive heart attack."

"How awful!" Nancy said.

"Yes. Dorothea changed after that. She became more—I don't know—more inward." Vanessa patted her light brown hair distractedly. "It was as if she was constantly wrestling with some deep

20

problem. Questions about life and death, I suppose."

Nancy turned as Maxine joined her and Vanessa. "Vanessa, you really have to read Dorothea's last book," Maxine said. "Kate gave me the manuscript today, and I read it all afternoon. It's very different from anything Dorothea ever did before."

"Last book?" Vanessa raised a questioning eyebrow. "What do you mean?"

"It's called *Crooked Heart*. It's the story of a perfect murder, told from the point of view of the murderer," Maxine explained. "I must say, it's very convincing. I'm sure it will cause a huge stir. It's a guaranteed best-seller."

Nancy noticed that some of the others had overheard and were moving closer.

"Hold on," Erika Olsen put in. There was an interested gleam in her blue eyes. "Are you talking about an unpublished manuscript by Dorothea? A completed work? That's mine!"

Bill Denton pushed into the group. "You're both out of line," he said. "I'm still the agent for Dorothea's works. Anything she wrote has to come through me."

"I'm sorry, Bill," Maxine said firmly. "I wasn't planning to mention this to anyone, but you've forced my hand. Shortly before she died, Dorothea told me she was planning to look for a new agent. She wasn't entirely happy with your handling of her royalty payments."

Bill's face turned bright red. "That's a lie!" he sputtered. "Dorothea owed her success to me. She said so herself!"

Maxine murmured something so softly that only Bill—and Nancy, who was standing next to her—could hear. "I taped the call," she said. *"All* of it."

In an instant Bill's face went from red to white. "I—I'll talk to you after dinner," he muttered to Maxine.

Before Nancy even had time to wonder what that was all about, Erika stepped forward to face Maxine. "I want that book," she demanded.

"I'm sure you do, dear," Maxine replied calmly. "But you can't have it."

Erika's left hand toyed nervously with the knot of her silk scarf. "Look," she said, "Dorothea promised it to me. I convinced her that Cameron & Sweazy could do more for her than your house, and she agreed to move."

"Then why didn't she?" Maxine asked sweetly.

"She died," Erika blurted out. "I had no idea that she'd finished the manuscript she promised me."

"You don't have a contract for it," Bill said. "Dorothea never signed a contract without my okay."

"No, I don't," Erika admitted. "But I bet Maxine doesn't, either. How did you get that manuscript, anyway?"

"That's my doing, I'm afraid," Kate said, putting her empty punch glass down on a nearby table. "After Dorothea died, I found a big envelope marked 'To My Editor.' There was a note attached from Dorothea, asking me to keep it safe and not deliver it until the Mystery Mansion museum was ready to open. I just assumed that 'My Editor' meant Maxine, so I gave her the envelope this morning."

"You should have given it to me," Bill said, frowning. "I'm her agent."

Nancy saw that the squabble had attracted George's and Patrick's attention, too. Catching George's glance, Nancy rolled her eyes. Vanessa Van Ness and Professor Coining had retreated to the couch, obviously uncomfortable with the conversation. Julian Romarain stood protectively next to Kate, who was trying to arbitrate.

"I'm afraid that I should have kept the manuscript and asked the Burden Foundation what to do with it," Kate said. "Dorothea left the rights to all her works to the foundation, so it owns this manuscript, too. Maxine, I'm sorry, but I'll have to ask you to give it back until we can resolve this."

"Of course, dear, I understand," Maxine said.

"But I can't possibly return it before I've found out all the sordid details of the murder! I'll bring it to you tomorrow morning."

"That'll be fine," Kate told her.

Just then a young man wearing black pants, a white shirt, and a bow tie slipped through the double doors near the fireplace, closing them behind him. Kate hurried over to him, obviously relieved to escape the argument over Dorothea's manuscript.

"Dinner is ready," she announced, pushing open the double doors that led to the dining room.

"I'm starved," George told Nancy as they joined the rear of the little crowd following Kate. "The last thing I ate was a—"

She broke off as those at the front of the group stopped short. Nancy heard gasps and exclamations from them.

"What's going on?" she asked. Even standing on tiptoe, she couldn't see over Vanessa Van Ness.

Finally the others stepped into the dining room and moved to one side. Nancy's mouth fell open when she saw what they were exclaiming about.

A long mahogany table set with fine porcelain, silver, and crystal occupied the center of the wood-paneled room. A dozen tall candles in three silver candelabra cast flickering light on the table, on the oil portraits on the wall—and on the still figure of a man in a butler's uniform lying on the floor.

The room was just bright enough for Nancy to make out the maroon silk cord knotted tightly around the man's neck.

Chapter

Three

GEORGE DUG her fingers into Nancy's arm. "Nancy!" she gasped. "Is he—"

"I don't know," Nancy replied, her throat suddenly very dry.

"We have to do something!" Vanessa exclaimed. She rushed forward and knelt next to the body. When she looked up, her face was red and she spoke angrily. "This is not a funny joke!"

Confused, Nancy glanced quickly at Patrick. There was no mistaking the amusement on his face. When she glanced back at the body, she noticed this time that there was something strange about the way it was positioned.

"Wait, everybody," Kate said, pushing forward to face the shocked group. "Let me explain."

"No, let me," Julian insisted, stepping up next to her and touching her hand for a moment. "What you see is not real," he told the group. "The 'body' on the floor is actually a dummy. Kate asked me to set up this and several other 'crimes' as tests of your detecting abilities."

"Rubbish," Professor Coining muttered loudly.

Ignoring the professor, Julian took an envelope from Kate and held it up. Nancy could see the Murder to Go skull in the upper left-hand corner.

"In here," Julian went on, "is a full explanation of the crime and its solution. You have five minutes to study the scene of the crime, without touching anything. Then we'll discuss it. The person who comes closest to the solution is the winner. Any questions?"

Professor Coining scowled. "Yes. Why are we wasting our time with this?" Obviously he had no interest in the challenge. Then again, he was an expert on mystery writing, Nancy recalled, not on mysteries themselves.

"Oh, come on, Marsden. Maybe this isn't so bad," Vanessa said. "Be a sport. This won't take long."

Under Julian's direction, the guests lined up and slowly filed past the dummy. While Nancy was waiting for her turn, she studied the rest of the room. Hanging in one corner was a maroon silk bellpull that ended in a ragged edge about six feet above the floor. A horn-handled carving knife lay on the floor just below the bellpull. On the sideboard, she spotted a case that contained a horn-handled carving fork and an empty space the size and shape of the knife. A heavy crystal decanter stood next to it on an engraved silver tray. The decanter had smudges around the neck and on one side.

"This is sort of fun," George whispered as she and Nancy moved closer to the dummy. She fell quiet when it was their turn to examine the crime scene.

Nancy studied the dummy, which was lying on its back, its head skewed to one side. It was dressed in gray- and black-striped trousers and a black swallowtail coat. A shaggy mustache dominated the face, and gray gloves covered its hands. Stooping down, Nancy examined the soles of the dummy's brown shoes. Dried mud was caked on the heels.

On the floor next to the dummy was a half-filled black cloth sack. An ornate silver teapot poked out of the sack, and half a dozen silver spoons and forks were scattered across the rug in front of it.

"Erika's turn," Julian said.

Nancy and George stepped out of the way.

"Do you have any ideas?" George whispered.

"A few," Nancy replied, smiling. "But I think I'll wait to see how the others solve the case."

Bill Denton was the last one in line. He glanced at the dummy, gave a snort, and said, "Simple."

"Does that mean you've solved the mystery?" Julian asked. He took a pen and a small notebook from his pocket.

"What mystery?" Bill scoffed. "It's obvious what happened. There was a burglary, and the butler was the inside man. He and his partner got into an argument, and his partner strangled him. End of story."

Julian made some notes, then asked, "Does anyone have any questions about Bill's theory?"

Nancy cleared her throat. "Yes," she said. "Why did the partner leave the loot behind?"

With a shrug, Bill replied, "He got spooked by something. He lost his head and ran."

"Why did he strangle the victim?" George spoke up. "Wouldn't it have been faster and easier to stab him with that carving knife?"

Good question, Nancy thought. And it was obviously one Bill Denton hadn't considered.

"How should I know?" the agent huffed. "Maybe he couldn't stand the sight of blood."

Erika was standing just behind Nancy. "I don't understand," she said, stepping forward. "What was the butler doing while the other guy was cutting down that bellpull? Just standing around waiting to be strangled?"

Bill scowled at her. "I never said I knew

everything about this stupid game. Have you got a better solution?"

"I'm not a detective, I'm an editor," Erika replied. She glanced at Patrick, obviously hoping to catch his attention, but he didn't seem to notice.

"How about the rest of you?" Julian asked. "Does anyone have a different solution?"

Nancy was pretty sure she knew the answer, but she didn't feel comfortable about being the first to come forward. There was an uncomfortable silence, until Vanessa Van Ness broke it. "Well, I did notice a few rather odd things," she said slowly.

"Yes?" Julian prompted.

"I suppose a butler might wear gray gloves, though white is more correct," she began. "And although butlers are almost always clean-shaven, it's possible that one might have a mustache. But a real butler would *never* wear brown shoes with his uniform. And certainly not brown shoes with mud on them. So I have to conclude that the victim was not a butler—he was merely disguised as a butler. Why? Because he was planning to rob the house. And judging by the bag of loot next to the body, he was in the middle of doing it when someone came upon him and killed him."

Julian smiled and made a few more notes.

"Yes, but who?" Erika asked impatiently.

"I think we can make an excellent guess,"

Vanessa replied. "Someone came in, carrying a heavy decanter on a silver tray. He spotted the burglar and knocked him out with the decanter. Then, overcome by a murderous rage, he took out the carving knife, cut down the bell cord, and strangled the unconscious burglar with it."

"That's just guesswork," Bill growled.

Vanessa shook her head. "Not quite. If the silver tray had been on the sideboard, the burglar would certainly have put it in his sack with the rest of the loot. So the killer must have brought it into the room. And the smudges on the decanter show that someone held it by the neck and hit something with it. I suspect that if we analyzed the side of the decanter, we'd find traces of hair cream."

"Bravo, Vanessa," Maxine put in. "I like that touch."

"Yes, but who did it?" Erika asked again.

"Isn't it obvious?" Vanessa's eyes twinkled as she took in the circle of faces. "If any of the rest of you know the answer, let's all say it together. One—two—three—"

Nancy joined the chorus of, "The butler did it!" Then everyone in the room cracked up— except Bill Denton.

"I still don't see why you think the butler did it," he grumbled.

Nancy couldn't resist speaking up. "The killer came in carrying the decanter on a tray," she explained. "When he saw the burglar from the back, dressed as the butler, he knew instantly that he was an imposter and bopped him with the decanter. He knew because he himself was the butler. Also, he knew where to find the carving knife, which he didn't think of as a weapon, because for him it was a tool for cutting things—like the bell cord. After he'd cooled off and realized what he'd done, he ran away."

Julian tore open the envelope with the solution in it and passed the paper inside to Kate, his hand lingering on hers a second longer than it had to. Kate read the paper.

"The winner is Vanessa Van Ness," she then announced. "I must add an honorable mention to Nancy Drew also."

As the applause died down, Julian and Patrick carried away the dummy and the props from the challenge. Nancy and George circled the table to find their name cards. Nancy was seated between Patrick and Bill, while George was across the table, between Vanessa and Julian.

Once Patrick and Julian had joined the rest of the group at the table, Nancy turned to Patrick and said, "That was fun. I just hope the real butler didn't find our game upsetting."

Patrick grinned at her. "Actually, there isn't one. Never was. Aunt Dotty made do with a cook-housekeeper, who retired after she died."

"What about her?" Nancy asked, nodding toward a young woman in a maid's uniform who was serving the soup.

"We hired her and three others, along with a cook, just for this conference," Patrick replied.

"I'm sure the museum will be a huge success," Nancy said. "Was your aunt planning it for a long time?"

Patrick chuckled. "If she was, she didn't tell anyone," he replied. "We were all surprised to hear about it when her will was read."

"All?" Nancy repeated. "Do you have a lot of relatives?"

"No, just me. I meant Kate and Mrs. Margolis —Aunt Dotty's housekeeper. And, of course, Maxine and Bill. My aunt had hinted that they'd be in her will. But she must have been worried about leaving enough money for the museum, so she made the gifts to her friends quite small. They must have thought they'd be remembered a little more generously than they were."

"You must have been disappointed, too," Nancy said. As the words left her mouth, she realized she was prying into personal territory. "Sorry— you don't have to answer that," she added quickly.

Patrick didn't seem to mind. He smiled and said, "I was surprised. We never talked about it, but I thought the estate would come to me. Still, turning Mystery Mansion into a museum was obviously close to my aunt's heart, so for her sake, I'm doing whatever I can to help bring it about. Besides, the foundation is giving me a decent salary and letting me live here for free while we get the place set up."

Smiling, Patrick smoothly changed the subject. "I've heard about some of the cases you've solved," he said. "How does George figure into your detective work?"

Nancy suppressed a grin. It was obviously George, not the cases, that Patrick was interested in.

She and Patrick turned as Erika spoke from the other side of Patrick. The editor didn't appear to be very happy about the attention Patrick was giving Nancy and George. Touching his arm, Erika said something in a sultry voice, too low for Nancy to hear. Patrick gave Nancy an apologetic smile and turned his attention back to Erika.

As the maid served their second course, roast beef with scalloped potatoes and string beans, Nancy turned to Bill Denton. For the rest of the meal, she listened to him brag about the great deals he'd negotiated for Dorothea's books.

Nancy was relieved when dinner was over and Kate announced, "Friends, this is an important moment for the Mystery Mansion Museum. In a few minutes we will install Dorothea Burden's unique collection of gold figurines in their new home. Will you all come with us to the display room?"

Nancy, George, and the others followed her back through the living room and into a long hallway. At the far end of the hall was a set of double doors, which Kate unlocked and pushed open.

"Please go in," she said. "We'll be right back." She beckoned to Patrick, and the two of them left the room.

"Nancy, look at this place!" George whispered. "Is all this stuff real?"

Good question, thought Nancy. A wooden gallows, complete with hangman's noose, stood in one corner, stretching almost to the high ceiling. Arranged on the walls were daggers and pistols of every sort, some of them obviously very old. A mannequin in the center of the room was dressed in an antique lace-trimmed costume. Sinister brown stains surrounded a small hole in the breast of the dress. Nancy couldn't suppress a small shiver.

Near the door was an empty glass display case that was lit by two small spotlights. Nancy and George joined the others in a semicircle around the case. When Patrick and Kate returned, Patrick was holding a leather box tooled in gold, about a foot wide, two feet long, and three inches thick.

Smiling at the group, Kate said, "We wanted to give you all a chance to see Dorothea's figurines up close before we put them in the display case. Patrick?"

Nancy and George leaned forward. From the brochure, Nancy knew the figurines were very special, not just for the gold and precious jewels they were made of, but also for the artistry and care that had gone into making them. She felt a tingle of anticipation as Patrick lifted the lid of the leather box with a flourish.

Vanessa Van Ness was the first to react. "It's empty!" she cried. "They're gone!"

Chapter

Four

NANCY COULD hardly believe her eyes. The rich blue velvet lining of the box was indented in about twelve places, each space ready to receive one statuette. All the spaces were now empty.

"Oh, no!" George said in a horrified voice.

Next to her, Patrick reacted as if he were in shock. He stood perfectly still and stared down into the box. After a moment of stunned silence, everyone started talking at once.

"Bravo, Julian," said Professor Coining. "For our after-dinner entertainment, I suppose you expect us to grill one another until we find out who stole the little trinkets."

Julian stared at the professor as if he had lost his mind. "I didn't arrange this," he said, nervously stroking his beard. "I never even saw the statues."

"Are you serious?" Erika asked dubiously. "This isn't another of your staged crimes?"

"Of course it isn't," Julian burst out.

"Maybe they were taken away to be cleaned or something," Bill Denton suggested. "You know —before they went on display."

He turned expectantly to Kate, but she hadn't seemed to hear him. Her face was taut with strain, and her eyes were still glued to the empty case.

Finally she blinked. "I promise they were in the safe in this box. Armand Wasserman—he's the foundation's president—insisted we keep them in a secure place."

"Who knows the combination?" Nancy asked.

"Nobody," Kate replied. "I mean, I do, and Armand, but nobody else. Why are you all staring at me that way? *I* didn't steal the figurines."

"Then whoever did must be an expert safecracker," Patrick said. "Aunt Dotty spent a lot of money on that safe. It's a good one."

The blood seemed to drain from Kate's face as she put her hands on the edge of the display case to stop herself from falling. Julian sprang up and helped her to a chair.

Nancy's mind was racing, her detective instincts on alert. "Who was the last person to see the figurines, and when?" she asked.

"I believe I was," Professor Coining said. "I had the privilege of examining them this morning. I intend to write a paper on the significance of those particular characters in Dorothea's books. I studied the figures for perhaps half an hour."

"Alone?" Nancy asked.

The professor hesitated, then said, "For some of the time, yes. But the figures were in their case when Kate returned it to the safe. Ask her, if you don't believe me."

"That's right," Kate confirmed. "I glanced inside, just to make sure all the figures were secure. They were."

Vanessa had been listening intently to the conversation. Now she asked, "When was this, dear?"

"Just before lunch. About noon, I guess."

"So the figures could have been stolen at any time between noon and now," Nancy pointed out.

"No, they couldn't," Maxine said. "I went into the study to read at around five o'clock, and I stayed there until our get-together in the living room. Nobody came in the whole time."

"And I was in and out of the study all afternoon, from just after lunch until around five," Kate added.

"We really need to get these times down as

exactly as possible," Nancy said. "When was 'just after lunch'?"

Kate thought for a moment. "I don't know— one-thirty?"

"Then it sounds as if the most likely time for the theft was between noon and one-thirty," Nancy said. "George and I are in the clear. We didn't even get here until nearly five. Anybody else?"

"The staff," Kate said. "They arrived in the middle of the afternoon, and none of them has ever been here before. I doubt if they've even heard of the figurines, and they certainly wouldn't know where they were kept."

"I arrived after five also," Erika said, obviously relieved.

"And so did I," Vanessa said. "Of course, any one of us could have paid an earlier visit secretly. . . ."

"Someone would have had to buzz you in," Kate pointed out. "Ordinarily, that someone is me, but with all the comings and goings this afternoon . . ."

"What times are we talking about?" Bill asked. "Noon to one-thirty? Let's see, I was on the phone with Leo Mallet, a client of mine in Chicago, from a little before noon until about one. He's a very talkative guy. Then I decided I had to talk to him in person, so I went out to my car."

40

"We went down together, remember?" Professor Coining put in. "I was walking along the hallway, and you cannoned into me as you left your room. I was on my way for a stroll on the grounds, so I walked you to the parking lot."

Bill Denton nodded. "I drove into Chicago, spent a little time with Leo, and drove straight back. I got here a little before five." Smiling, he added, "I guess I've got an alibi."

"I don't," Julian said, glowering. "I didn't go into the study, but I was all over the rest of the house, setting up the mystery challenges for the weekend."

With a shrug, Maxine said, "Don't fret. I don't have one either, and I already admitted that I spent time alone in the study. That doesn't mean I'm a thief."

Nancy had been listening carefully to the other guests. Was one of them a thief? It certainly seemed like it, but which one? This wasn't going to be an easy case to solve—all the suspects were mystery experts!

"What about the police?" George asked. "Shouldn't we call them and report the theft?"

"I don't think we should rush to do that," Kate said. "I'd like to find out what Armand thinks before we bring officials in. With a distinguished group like this, we ought to be able to solve the crime and recover the figures without a scandal."

Nancy studied her curiously, but Kate wouldn't meet her eyes.

"I think we should report the theft," Nancy said, "but I'm a guest here. It's not up to me to decide."

"What about searching the house?" Patrick suggested.

"It'd be a waste of time," Julian said, rolling his eyes. "A place this size, we could search for weeks and still miss something as small as those figurines." After an uneasy silence, he added, "If nobody minds, I'm going to turn in early."

There were murmurs of agreement from some of the others.

Taking a deep breath, Kate said, "All right. I've decided to ask Nancy Drew if she'll take charge of investigating the theft. I'm sure you all know her reputation as a detective. If any of you think of anything that might help solve it, please tell her right away."

Nancy was surprised. Of course she was ready to help in any way she could, but it would have been nice if Kate had asked her before making that announcement. Warning all the suspects that she was on the case wasn't going to make her task any easier either!

As people began to leave for their rooms George approached Nancy, her hands in her pockets. "What now? Should we start a search for the figures?" she asked.

Nancy shook her head. "Julian's right. Even a team of experts would need days to do a thorough search of a place this size. I would like to check out that safe, though."

The two girls went over to Kate, who was still standing next to the empty display case. When Nancy explained what she wanted, Kate smiled and said, "No problem. Dorothea's study is on this floor, in the west wing. It's the last doorway on the left. You'll need the key."

"You mean the study is kept locked?" Nancy asked.

Kate's cheeks turned pink and her gaze shifted around the room. "Usually," she said, "but this afternoon I was in and out so much that it seemed silly to keep locking it."

"What about between noon and one-thirty?" Nancy asked. "Was it locked then?"

Kate hesitated. Finally she said, "I think so, but I'm not absolutely sure. I'm sorry." She handed Nancy the key.

"There's so little to go on," George said as she and Nancy went to the study. "I hope we find something in the safe."

The study was a cozy room, with a small fireplace, an antique desk, a reading chair, some oak bookcases, and a wooden file cabinet. The safe was built low into the wall, hidden behind a cabinet door that now stood ajar.

Nancy and George knelt down and studied the

safe. "There's no sign of tampering on the door," George pointed out. "Whoever opened it must have known the combination."

"Not necessarily," Nancy told her. "This sort of lock is hard to crack but not impossible for an expert. The question is, who around here—"

"Shh! Listen!" George put her hand on Nancy's arm while she cocked her head to one side.

There *was* something, Nancy realized. It sounded like the murmur of distant voices. But where was it coming from?

Suddenly the murmur grew louder and she could make out a few menace-filled words.

"I know what you did," the voice said. "I know, and I'm going to make sure you don't get away with it!"

Chapter

Five

THE VOICE fell silent as mysteriously as it had begun.

Nancy and George stared at each other, wide-eyed. When George started to say something, Nancy held her index finger to her lips as a warning to be silent. She scanned the room. The voice had seemed to come from near Dorothea's desk. Nancy crooked a finger to George, and the two of them began to tiptoe in that direction.

Suddenly a noise came from beyond the desk. It sounded like a door closing, followed by the click of a lock. It seemed to come from near a small table set against the wall. The table was bare.

Frowning, Nancy knelt down and peered under the table, then motioned for George to do the same. Set into the base of the wall was a louvered heating vent. The voice had obviously traveled through the heating duct from some other room.

Nancy touched George's shoulder and pointed to the door of the room. She didn't want to say anything, in case their voices traveled back through the vent to the other person, giving them away.

Once outside Nancy told George her theory, then asked, "Did you recognize that voice?"

George shook her head. "To tell the truth, I'm not even sure it was a man or a woman." She was worried when she asked, "Do you think the person was talking to us?"

"I doubt it," Nancy replied. "He or she would have to know we were in the study just now *and* know which heating duct came in there. No, my hunch is that we overheard someone threatening to expose the person who stole Dorothea's gold figurines. If we only knew where the voices came from and who was talking to whom, we could probably crack this case."

She started to add something, but a yawn took her by surprise. Glancing at her watch, she said, "It's too late to track them down now, though. We'd better turn in. Tomorrow I want to hunt down the plans of the house and trace that duct."

On Saturday morning Nancy awoke when a sunbeam slid through the crack between the velvet curtains and hit her face. She rolled over and covered her head with the pillow, but it was too late. She was awake.

Seeing that George was still sound asleep, Nancy got quietly out of bed and dressed in jeans and a turtleneck. She grabbed her leather jacket and tiptoed out of the room. It was still early, before eight. Maybe a walk in the garden would help her to think clearly about the theft of the jeweled figurines.

She left the mansion by way of the sun room and walked through the rose garden toward the end of the house that was under repair. It was a perfect Indian summer day—the sky was a flawless blue, and the sun was beginning to take the early-morning chill from the air. Nancy breathed in the scent of rich loam and dew-wet grass.

As she walked past the side of the house, she noticed what looked like the entrance to an old-fashioned maze. She strolled over to it. The boxwood hedges that made up the walls hadn't been trimmed in a while. Just inside the entrance, some of the branches were broken, making the maze look like a thicket.

Nancy decided that exploring the maze could wait for another time. In spite of the rising sun, the hedges were too dark and cold to be inviting.

Nancy wound around a pile of lumber, making her way toward the front corner of the mansion. She paused next to a flagstone path that made its way between flower beds that were ablaze with autumn color. Nancy followed the path down into a hollow with a tiny stream at the bottom. The house was out of sight now, hidden by the rise. Ahead, a set of stone steps led up to the white summerhouse she had glimpsed from her room the day before.

As she started up the steps, one of the summerhouse windows reflected a blinding flash of sunlight into Nancy's eyes, causing her to stumble. She closed her eyes until the black spots faded from her field of vision, then shaded her face with her hand and looked curiously up at the summerhouse. None of the windows caught the sun now.

Hmm, that's odd, Nancy thought. She took a step to each side, but still the windows mirrored only sky. What had caused that flash? Had a window been shifted by the breeze? There didn't appear to be any breeze, though, judging by the motionless branches of the trees near her.

Nancy shrugged and started up the steps again. The world was full of mysteries. She couldn't expect to solve all of them.

Near the top of the steps, she stopped short. She watched as the door to the summerhouse was pulled open from the inside, squeaking as it went.

Nancy recognized Erika's short blond hair as the young editor backed out of the summerhouse to pull the door shut. Erika hitched the handles of a canvas tote bag higher up on her shoulder and turned. When she saw Nancy, she gasped.

"You startled me! I didn't know anyone was here."

"Sorry, I didn't mean to scare you," Nancy said with a smile. "It's good to know I'm not the only early riser. Pretty day, isn't it?"

Erika peered around her absently. "Yes, it is. Chilly, though," she said. She bent down to brush a patch of dust from her navy blue skirt, then buttoned her matching blazer.

Nancy decided to ask a few roundabout questions. Maybe she could uncover some clue to the theft of the figurines. "It's fascinating being here at Mystery Mansion," she said lightly. "Did you know Dorothea well?"

"I certainly did," Erika replied. "I started writing her fan letters when I was still in high school. The amazing part is, she answered them. In college, I organized the Dorothea Burden Society and invited her to come speak to the members. That was the first time we met in person."

"But not the last," Nancy guessed as they started back toward the main house. Erika seemed to take a lot of pride in her relationship with the late novelist.

Erika gave a smug smile. "Not at all," she said. "I even spent a couple of weekends here at

Mystery Mansion. Dotty loved to give her guests guided tours."

Nancy said, "You must know the house really well then. It's—well—it's very unusual."

Erika stopped walking abruptly and turned to meet Nancy's eyes. "You've heard about the secret passages, haven't you?" she demanded. "Here's some free advice. Stay away from them. They can be really dangerous, even for people who know their way around in them. And there aren't many of us now that Dotty's gone."

"I'll remember that," Nancy said. She wondered why Erika had become so unfriendly.

They were making their way past what looked like a gardener's shed, when something purple and green came hurtling around a corner of the shed and slammed into Erika. She crashed to the ground, and her tote bag went flying.

"Oh, I'm sorry," Patrick said, catching his breath. "I was jogging and wasn't paying attention to where I was going."

Erika seemed dazed as Patrick and Nancy helped her up. She glanced around at the scattered contents of her tote bag, then started scuttling around picking up what appeared to be hundreds of typed pages.

"Oh, thanks," Erika said breathlessly as Nancy and Patrick bent to help her. Taking bunches of pages from them, she stuffed them hurriedly in the tote bag. "I brought a manuscript with me to work on this weekend. I hoped to steal some time before breakfast today."

"What's this for?" Nancy asked, picking up a black flashlight that had also fallen out of the bag. "Were you worried that you wouldn't have enough light to read by?"

Erika reddened. "I always carry a flashlight," she said defensively. "I have problems with the dark."

Nancy studied her through narrowed eyes. The editor was definitely hiding something, and Nancy was determined to find out what it was.

"Look who has attached herself to Patrick," George said to Nancy in a low voice a half hour later. The two girls were just entering the dining room, where a buffet-style breakfast had been set up.

Nancy noticed Erika learning close to Patrick at one end of the table, toast and coffee in front of her.

"Not that you care, right, George?" Nancy teased, fixing herself a bowl of cereal and fruit.

George raised her head from the eggs and bacon she was spooning onto her plate. "I really don't—not the way you mean, anyway. He is a nice guy, and she's so . . ."

"Whiny?" Nancy supplied. "Well, I'm sure Patrick knows how to take care of himself. Come on, we've got a case to solve."

The two girls sat down next to Vanessa, who was sitting across from Kate and Julian Romarain. Professor Coining and Bill Denton were also there, sharing a newspaper.

Turning to Vanessa, Nancy said, "You knew Dorothea Burden very well, didn't you?"

"Yes, I did."

"What did you think when you heard about her will?" Nancy continued.

Vanessa took a sip of coffee before answering. "You mean that she had left everything to the foundation?" she said. "Well, all her friends were surprised. I guess none of us expected her to cut Patrick off the way she did. She had always treated him as if he were her own son. Personally, I think she may have become just a tiny bit gaga toward the end."

The conversation ended as Kate tapped a fork against her water glass. "Good morning, everyone," Kate said. "As you know, our first event this morning is an informal talk by Maxine Treitler, entitled 'Editing Dorothea.' That will take place right after breakfast, in the library."

From outside came the sound of tires on gravel, followed by the slamming of car doors.

"Oh, good," Kate added. "That must be the minivan with the participants who are staying in town. I'll go welcome them and show them to the library. Please join us there as soon as you're done."

Nancy and George hurriedly ate their breakfasts. Taking their coffee cups with them to the library, they found a dozen newcomers gathered around a big oak table, enjoying coffee and pastries. Wooden shelves filled with leather-bound books lined the walls, and reading chairs were scattered throughout the room. Kate was passing out name tags, introducing people to one another, and urging everyone to take a seat for Maxine's talk.

Professor Coining was standing near Nancy, holding a pastry on a paper napkin. When Kate suggested he sit down, he replied, "Yes, of course. As soon as our speaker arrives."

Kate seemed surprised. "Isn't Maxine here?" she asked, glancing around the room.

"I haven't seen her yet today," Nancy said.

"She wasn't at breakfast," George added.

"Oh, no, she must have overslept," Kate moaned. "Nancy, would you mind running up to her room and reminding her about her talk? She's in the Rue Morgue room. You can't miss it. I'd go myself, but I have to stay and play social director."

"I'll go with you," Patrick offered.

The two of them went upstairs and down the hall. He stopped at a door with a small blue enamel plaque that said Rue Morgue. He tapped on the door. There was no answer.

Patrick knocked harder. This time the latch

clicked and the door swung open an inch or two. Nancy met Patrick's startled gaze.

"I'll wait here," he said with a smile. "If Maxine has overslept, she might be scared to find a man in her room."

"Okay." Nancy pushed the door open a little wider. "Maxine? Are you here?" she called. "It's Nancy Drew."

Silence.

"I'll take a look," she told Patrick. Stepping inside, she saw that the room was empty, and the curtains were open. "Maxine?" Nancy said again. Then she called back to Patrick, "There's no one here."

He followed her in. "The bathroom door is open, and the light's on," he pointed out.

Nancy crossed the room to the other side of the bed—and pulled up short. Her hands flew to her mouth. "Oh, no!"

Maxine was lying faceup on the carpeted floor. She was wearing a blue dress and matching blue pumps. Her eyes were open wide, staring at nothing. One look at the bruises on her throat told Nancy what had happened.

Maxine was dead. Someone had strangled her.

Chapter
Six

PATRICK STARED PAST Nancy and took a deep breath. Is she—?"

"I'm afraid so." Nancy turned away from the body with a shudder. Her mind instantly raced into action. "Go downstairs, tell Kate what happened, and ask her to get the police here right away, okay?" she told Patrick. "I'll stay here and make sure nothing is disturbed. Oh—and please don't touch the doorknob on the way out of the room. The killer might have been careless enough to leave fingerprints. Tell everyone to remain downstairs."

"Sure, right away," Patrick said. He seemed glad to have an excuse to leave the room.

As soon as he was gone, Nancy made a note of

the time—9:27. Taking a deep breath, she forced herself to take a good look around.

In the bathroom, one of the towels was hung neatly on the rack, but the other was rumpled and damp. Droplets of water remained in the bathtub. On the ledge over the bathroom sink were several containers of makeup. The lid of a small jar of foundation was resting on the jar, not screwed down. A blush compact was also open, and its brush lay in the sink, where it had apparently fallen.

The evidence told a clear story. Earlier that morning Maxine had showered, then gotten dressed. As she was making up her face, someone had crept in. Maxine must have heard the intruder and gone into the bedroom, where she was strangled.

Nancy turned her attention to the bedroom. Several thin file folders, a legal pad, and a pair of reading glasses all rested on the desk. Nancy was able to make out the names on the folders without touching them, but none of them meant anything to her.

She frowned as a thought struck her. Maxine hadn't seemed like the kind of person who would leave her door unlocked while she showered and dressed. Hurrying over to the door, Nancy saw that the spring lock was set to lock the door any time it was closed. The only reason she and Patrick had been able to get in was that the last person to leave—presumably the murderer—hadn't pulled the door closed all the way.

How then had the killer gotten *into* the room?

In this house there was one obvious possibility. Nancy's gaze flew to the closet. The door was ajar, so she went through it sideways, careful not to touch anything. As in the room she and George were in, the closet walls were made of closely fitted cedar planks. Nancy soon noticed one section of boards that wasn't even with the others. It appeared to be set back slightly into the wall.

Nancy hurried back into the room and found a pencil. She pushed with the eraser end on the odd section of wall. Strictly speaking, she shouldn't have touched anything at all, but she knew that what she was doing wouldn't mess up any evidence.

"Yes!" she whispered. The recessed section of closet wall had swung open to reveal a hidden passage. Dust coated most of the floor, but some of it was scuffed. When Nancy bent down to study the surface from an angle, she saw several blurred footprints and one that was clear and sharp. It was from a woman's shoe that had an unusual pattern of ripples across the sole. She did her best to memorize the pattern, then returned to the bedroom, leaving the secret panel ajar.

Five minutes later the police arrived. The first one to enter the room was a young uniformed officer whose eyes darted around the room, pausing only briefly on Nancy. Just behind him was a slightly older person, a woman in a sergeant's uniform. She nodded to Nancy and took up a position at one side of the door.

The last to enter was a man of about forty with big ears, an easy smile, and dark hair that flopped over his eyes. He was dressed in a bright-colored running suit. Nancy guessed that the call about Maxine's murder had interrupted his Saturday morning at home.

"You must be Nancy Drew," he said, and smiled easily. "I've heard of you. I'm Lieutenant Kitridge. What have you got for us?"

Nancy quickly described finding Maxine's body. While she spoke he took a look at the corpse. Then he sent the young man downstairs to call headquarters and posted the sergeant outside the door.

Returning to Nancy, he asked, "What made you and Mr. Burden come up here? Did you have a particular reason to be worried about the deceased?"

Nancy told him about the lecture Maxine had been scheduled to give. "There's something else, too," she added. "Last night a set of valuable jeweled figurines disappeared." Now that there had been a murder, Nancy knew she couldn't keep the theft from the police.

The lieutenant gave Nancy a skeptical look.

"You mean they were stolen?" When Nancy nodded, he said, "Didn't it occur to anyone to call the police?"

"I urged Kate Jefferson to call you last night," Nancy replied. "She's the executive secretary of the Burden Foundation. She felt she ought to consult her boss first."

The lieutenant shook his head. "Afraid of a scandal, right?" he said. "Same old story. Now, would you mind giving me a quick rundown on all those people downstairs? What's going on here?"

When Nancy told him about the conference, the lieutenant rubbed his chin. "We're going to have to put the conference on hold," he said. "The people who arrived here at nine had better go back to town. None of them could have done it because the victim was killed before nine."

He went to the door and spoke briefly to the sergeant. Then he turned back to Nancy. "I'm going to have to talk to everyone who stayed here last night. Okay, Ms. Drew, I'll see you again after I've gathered a few more facts about this case."

Nancy hesitated. "If you like, maybe I can give you a hand," she offered. "I am on the inside, here."

"Sounds like a good idea," he replied after a moment. "Off the record, of course. Like I said, I've heard about your skills as a detective, and this is already starting to look like a very tricky case. I may need all the help I can get. Patrick Burden told us to use the library downstairs when he greeted us at the door a few minutes ago. That's where we'll be and I'll call you if I need you."

Downstairs, Nancy found the other house-guests gathered in the living room. Julian was arranging kindling and logs in the big fireplace. Everyone else was sitting and watching. No one was talking. At the sound of Nancy's footsteps, they all turned to her.

"Nancy!" Erika exclaimed, nervously fingering the neck of her blouse. "Patrick said we had to stay here. Is it true? Is Maxine—"

Nancy nodded. "I'm afraid so."

"It must have been a burglar," Kate said. Her eyes were red, and her fingers were tearing a tissue into tiny bits. "Yes, of course, that must be it! First he stole the figurines, then he murdered Maxine."

It was reasonable that Kate would be upset, but Nancy had to wonder if Kate knew more than she was telling.

"Why?" Professor Coining asked coolly. "I understand why someone might steal those gold figures. They were quite valuable. But why would any burglar hang around the scene of the crime all night, then wantonly kill a middle-aged book editor?"

The same thought had been troubling Nancy, too. Before anyone could comment further, the police sergeant appeared in the living-room doorway.

Glancing at a slip of paper in her hand, she said, "Mr. Coining? The lieutenant would like a word with you, sir. Will you come with me, please?"

There was a brief, charged silence after the professor left. Finally Patrick said, "They're planning to 'sir' and 'please' him until he confesses. A typical example of police brutality."

"How can you make jokes at a time like this!" Kate burst out. "Poor Maxine is lying dead upstairs, and the figurines are gone. This scandal could destroy everything we're trying to do here at Mystery Mansion. I don't see what's funny about that!"

A silence fell over the room and continued as each guest was taken off to be interviewed. Finally the sergeant appeared in the doorway for the last time and beckoned to Nancy. "Lieutenant Kitridge would like to see you now."

Nancy followed the sergeant to the library. When she entered, Lieutenant Kitridge was standing behind the room's big oak table. He was leaning on his two hands, studying pages of notes that were spread across the tabletop. Seeing Nancy, he straightened up and said, "Well, Ms. Drew, this is a tricky one."

"Please call me Nancy, Lieutenant."

"Nancy, then," he said. He gestured toward a clear plastic bag that contained a flowered scarf. "Have you seen that before?"

The scarf looked familiar, but Nancy couldn't place it. "I *think* so," she said. "Is that what——?"

"Yep," he said with a nod. "We found it under the deceased. We're ninety-five percent sure it's the murder weapon. As soon as we examine the fibers we found under the victim's fingernails, I'm betting it'll be one hundred percent."

"Did anyone identify it?" Nancy asked.

The lieutenant shook his head. "Not in so many words. But some of the guests obviously recognized it."

"Do you have anything on the time of death?"

"We won't have the medical examiner's report until tomorrow," the lieutenant replied. "But his assistant did the preliminary exam. His guess was that the victim was killed somewhere around eight o'clock."

That pretty much fit with what Nancy had guessed already. "Did the murderer get in by the secret passage?" she asked.

"It looks that way," Lieutenant Kitridge replied. "Secret passages? Whoever built this place was obviously a nut.

"What about motive? Any ideas?" he asked.

Nancy told him about the conversation she and George had overheard the night before. "If that was Maxine's voice," she concluded, "she may have discovered who stole the figurines and threatened the person with exposure."

"Or tried a little blackmail," Kitridge suggested. "That's a dangerous game when you're dealing with someone who's desperate."

He let out a weary sigh. "Why don't you go back to the others, Nancy? We've got a lot of routine stuff to wrap up here."

When Nancy rejoined the group in the living room, Kate was just announcing that lunch had been set up in the dining room.

While the others went through the double doors, Nancy took George aside to fill her in on what Lieutenant Kitridge had told her.

"So we still don't have a clue to who could have killed Maxine," George said as she and Nancy went into the dining room.

Nancy shook her head, then turned her attention to the spread of salads and sandwiches on the buffet. She and George were just sitting down next to Erika, when Bill Denton came over.

"Well, Erika," he said loudly. "I notice you're not wearing that flowered silk scarf of yours. What's the matter? Did you forget to unwind it from Maxine's neck?"

Chapter

Seven

Erika's face went completely white. Everyone at the table was silent and staring at her.

"It's not true," Erika murmured, barely above a whisper. "It's not!"

"Why else would that slick cop show me your scarf and ask if I'd ever seen it before?" Bill continued. "Did you admit it was yours?"

"I—" Erika swallowed, then said, "I told him it looked like one I have. But the store where I bought it sells thousands of those scarves every year. It's a classic."

"A classic piece of evidence, you mean," Bill said with a nasty grin.

Blinking furiously, Erika pushed back her chair and ran out of the room.

"That was a rotten thing to do, Bill," Vanessa

spoke up from the other side of the table. "I can understand why Dorothea decided to get a new agent."

Bill turned red. "That's a lie! I was her agent right to the end." He glared at Vanessa, then stalked out of the room, slamming the double doors behind him.

"Well, well," Professor Coining said with a chuckle. "This weekend is starting to resemble a classic mystery story in which the guests are picked off one by one. I suppose we should excuse Mr. Denton. From what I hear, he's having financial problems."

Nancy glanced sharply at the professor. He had to understand that he had just given Bill a motive for stealing the figurines. Had he just done it to divert attention away from himself?

Her thoughts were interrupted by Vanessa's standing up. "Sorry, I don't really have any appetite," she said, excusing herself.

"I don't, either," George added. "How about you, Nan?"

"I'm done," Nancy said.

As the two girls got up, Patrick announced, "We've put the conference on hold, of course. We hope you'll stay on at least through tomorrow, in case we're able to resume."

"Anyway, the police probably wouldn't like it if we decided to leave," Nancy pointed out.

Out in the hall she turned to George and said,

"Let's see if anyone's in the library still. We need someplace to talk."

The room was empty. Sunlight poured in through the french windows, illuminating the wooden bookcases.

"Well," George said as they sat down at the long table Lieutenant Kitridge had been using earlier. "Here we are with two crimes to solve, a theft and a murder. To think I was expecting a nice, relaxed weekend!"

"Two crimes, yes—but how many criminals?" Nancy asked. "Two? Or one?" She pulled a pad and pen out of her purse and started to jot down her thoughts.

George stared at her. "One? You mean Kate's idea, that a burglar came in, stole the figurines, and then waited around to kill Maxine?"

"Not quite like that," Nancy said. "But what if Maxine found out who the thief was and threatened to expose him or her?"

"Of course," George said excitedly. "And that's why she was killed—to silence her. Nancy! That mysterious voice we heard last night! What did it say? 'I know what you did, and I'll make sure you don't get away with it.' Wasn't that it?"

"Something like that," Nancy agreed.

"What if that was Maxine, speaking to whoever stole the gold figurines?"

Nancy nodded slowly. "Lieutenant Kitridge

and I were thinking the same thing. I just had another idea, right now."

George raised her eyebrows questioningly.

"Remember last night when Maxine got into that argument with Bill? She was hinting that he'd been embezzling money from Dorothea. Bill was very upset to hear that she had a taped conversation with Dorothea. What if he went to her room last night to talk to her? She could have been telling him that she knew he'd been stealing from Dorothea."

George slapped her palm on the table. "Sure! So he killed her to make sure she'd never tell anyone else about it."

"It fits," Nancy said. "But it's all just supposition. What about that scarf and the footprint I found in the secret passage? What we need to do now is find out whether the heating duct in Dorothea's study is somehow connected to the one in Maxine's room. There should be a plan around somewhere, but it might take us months to find it. I wonder if Kate could get us one."

Both girls looked up as the door opened slightly. Erika peeked in, then slipped into the library and shut the door behind her.

"Nancy, you've got to help me!" she said in a low, urgent voice. "The police are going to arrest me for murdering Maxine, I just know it!"

Seeing how distraught Erika was, George said, "Please sit down—here, next to me."

The blond editor did and took a deep breath to try to calm herself. "I know what you all think, but it's not true. I didn't kill her!"

"Then why do you think the police are going to arrest you?" Nancy asked.

Erika glanced down at her hands. "That scarf," she said. "Bill Denton was right—it *is* mine. Or at least, it's just like mine and mine's missing."

"How did it get into Maxine's room?" George asked gently.

"I don't know!"

Nancy checked out Erika's feet. She was wearing soft black shoes. Nancy couldn't see the soles, but she decided to take a chance.

"There's more to this than you're telling us," she told Erika. "You were in Maxine's room this morning, weren't you? And I know how you got in. By the secret passage."

Erika stared as if Nancy had just sprouted wings and a tail. "How—? You can't know that!"

"Yes, I can. And I imagine the police found the same clues that I noticed this morning."

"Fingerprints?" Erika said almost to herself. "I thought I was being so careful—"

"So, you admit it!" George exclaimed. She edged away from the young woman.

"I'm not a murderer!" Erika insisted. "I'm a thief. There, I said it!"

"*You* stole the figurines?" George asked.

"Figurines?" Erika repeated, puzzled. "No, no. *Crooked Heart*—the manuscript for Dorothea's last book. I couldn't sleep because I kept thinking about it. So early this morning I crept into Maxine's room and lifted the manuscript from her bedside table."

Nancy watched the editor carefully when she asked, "Where was Maxine? Asleep?"

Erika shook her head. "Her bed was empty. The bathroom door was closed, and I could hear the shower running. It's not like I stuck around to chat or anything. I just grabbed the manuscript and ran back into the secret passage."

"What time was that?" George asked.

Erika tugged at a lock of short, blond hair. "Eight? Just a little before I met you in the garden."

In her mind Nancy played back her meeting with Erika. "So that was Dorothea's manuscript that fell out of your tote bag?" she guessed.

"Yes. I nearly died! I was sure you'd see what it was."

"What about your scarf?" George asked, leaning forward in her chair. "Were you wearing it when you went to Maxine's room?"

Erika hesitated. "I—I might have been. I don't remember. Do you think the killer found it there and used it to frame me?"

"That's one possibility," Nancy replied. She

didn't bother to mention the more obvious one —that Maxine had discovered Erika in her room, and Erika, in a panic, had strangled her.

"I didn't kill her!" Erika repeated as if she knew what Nancy was thinking. "But I *know* they're going to arrest me. Will you help? You're the only one here I can turn to."

"I'll do my best to get to the bottom of Maxine's murder," Nancy hedged. "If you're innocent, the best way we can prove it is to find out who's guilty."

"Oh, thank you!"

"But," she added, holding up her hand, "I need your full cooperation. For starters, I want that manuscript. I'll see that Kate gets it back."

For half an instant Erika looked as if she might say no. Then she sighed, stood up, and said, "Okay, let's go."

Erika's room was decorated like a set from a 1920s detective movie. She walked straight across the room to a mirrored vanity table and pulled open the center drawer. She froze, staring down into it.

"Oh, no!" she said in a horrified whisper. "It's gone! Somebody stole it!"

Nancy and George ran to Erika's side. Sure enough, the drawer was empty.

"You're positive this is where you left it?" Nancy asked. "Could you have remembered wrong?"

"It was in this drawer," Erika insisted, rapping her knuckles on the vanity.

Nancy studied Erika's face. She was obviously distressed, but that didn't mean she was telling the truth. Nancy was about to probe further when there was a tap on the door. Lieutenant Kitridge poked his head inside.

"Ms. Olsen? I've been looking for you," he said. "I'm sorry, but I have to ask you to come with me. A number of questions have come up about your part in the death of Maxine Treitler."

Erika stared wordlessly at the police officer. Then her eyes rolled upward, and almost in slow motion, she started to slump to the floor.

Chapter

Eight

As ERIKA's KNEES crumpled, Nancy and George reached out to stop her from falling. Lieutenant Kitridge called over his shoulder to the hallway. "Sergeant Wilensky? Give me a hand, will you?"

Erika's eyes fluttered open after a moment. She stared dazedly at Nancy and George, who were still holding her up. The sergeant Nancy had seen that morning came in, and the three of them helped Erika into a chair. "Put your head down in your lap," the sergeant advised. "It helps to get the blood back to your brain."

After a few minutes Erika was sitting up and the color had returned to her cheeks.

"Are you okay, Ms. Olsen?" the lieutenant asked.

Erika nodded and got to her feet to start for the door. As she was leaving the room, she turned to Nancy with an imploring look.

With a frown Lieutenant Kitridge asked, "Are you starting to take sides, Nancy?"

Nancy shook her head. "I'll tell you what I told Erika. The best way to show she's innocent, if she is, will be to find out who's guilty."

"Her scarf was the murder weapon," Kitridge said. "The fibers we found under the victim's fingernails match. And I'm willing to bet those shoes she's wearing will match up with that footprint we found in the hidden passage."

"She admitted that she went to Maxine's room this morning," Nancy told him.

The lieutenant stared at Nancy with narrowed eyes. "You'd better tell me about that," he said.

When she'd finished, Kitridge rubbed his chin. "So now she says the manuscript is missing from her room," he said. "Do you buy that story?"

"I don't know," Nancy said truthfully. "She certainly wanted the manuscript badly enough to steal it. Maybe she's hidden it somewhere and intends to retrieve it later."

"If the evidence against her keeps piling up this way," the lieutenant said grimly, " 'later' for her is going to be a whole lot later. Figure twenty years to life."

With that, Lieutenant Kitridge left.

"Oh, I left my notes down in the library,"

Nancy said to George. The two girls made their way back downstairs. Nancy retrieved the notebook, then crossed over to the long windows to look outside.

A dark-colored sedan was just pulling out of the driveway. Sergeant Wilensky was driving with Erika in the backseat beside Lieutenant Kitridge. "There they go," Nancy said.

George didn't answer. When Nancy swung around George wasn't there. At the far end of the library a narrow door set between two carved bookcases was standing partially open, though.

Nancy started for the door, but before she reached it, the door swung wide open and George reappeared. She had a folded piece of blue paper in her hand and a grin on her face.

"Where were you?" Nancy asked. "What's that?"

"I decided to check out where that door goes," George replied. "It leads into Dorothea Burden's study. Now look what I found in her file cabinet—a blueprint of the heating system."

"Great!" Nancy helped unfold the large sheet of paper, and together they studied the diagram.

"Here's the library," George said, pointing. "And this must be the heating duct. It comes up directly from the main duct in the basement, right below us. And from here, it goes up to the second floor—"

"'R.M. room,'" Nancy read, squinting at the faint printing. "Rue Morgue—Maxine's room!"

George let out a low whistle. "So, our guess must be right. That mysterious voice last night *was* Maxine's."

Nancy nodded her agreement. "Which means, if we can find out who stole the figurines, there's a good chance we'll have found Maxine's murderer at the same time."

"Let's think about everyone's alibi," George said. "What are the important times again?"

Nancy's brow furrowed as she thought back. "According to Kate and the professor, the figures went back into the safe at noon," she said. "And at eight they were gone. The study was empty, and maybe locked, from noon to one-thirty. It was unlocked from one-thirty on, but Kate was in and out a lot. From about five until we got together before dinner, Maxine was in there alone."

"So unless the figurines were stolen by Kate or Maxine, they were probably taken between noon and one-thirty," George said. "Do you remember where people said they were during those times?"

"I'm not sure," Nancy admitted. "Maybe we'd better talk to everyone again and try to pin down where they were."

As they came out of the library, Nancy saw

Patrick at one of the doors down the hall. He had his back to her, and he seemed to be fiddling with the lock. Just as she and George drew near, he straightened up and the door swung open.

"Hi," Nancy called.

Patrick stiffened, pulling the door quickly closed again. He turned and gave them a dazzling smile. "Hello," he said, slipping a large key into his pocket. "Did you hear about Erika?" he asked.

"We were with her when the police took her in for questioning," George replied. Nodding toward the door, she said, "That's the display room, isn't it?"

"That's right," Patrick said.

"I didn't really get a chance to inspect the displays last night," George said. "Do you think we could take a peek?"

"Maybe later," he said with another big smile. "I was just locking up."

He shook the door handle, to make sure it was closed. Then he took the key from his pocket and turned it in the lock.

"We're still checking into the theft of the figures," Nancy told him. "Can you tell us where you were yesterday, from noon on?"

"Let me see. Julian and I got together with Kate at about twelve-fifteen to work out the details of some of the staged crimes for the weekend. We did that until about two. After that

I was alone for a while. At about four Professor Coining and I had a cup of tea together, and I stayed with him until Bill and you came a little before five. From then on, I was with someone every moment until Kate and I went to get the figures from the safe."

Nancy said, "Thanks, Patrick."

As they moved away, George whispered, "He lied to us, Nancy! He wasn't closing that room, he was opening it."

"I noticed," Nancy whispered back. "I wonder why?"

The girls peered into an empty living room before continuing on to the sun room. Professor Coining was there, stretched out on a chaise longue. An open book was resting on his stomach, his eyes closed.

"Professor Coining," Nancy said softly.

He awoke with a start, and his eyes darted around the sun room. "Hmm? Yes, what is it?"

Nancy asked her question. The professor told her that he had eaten a sandwich with Kate and Maxine from noon to twelve-thirty. He had walked Bill to his car at around one and had had tea with Patrick at four. "In other words, young lady, you could drive a truck through the holes in my alibi," he concluded with a chuckle.

After tracking down Julian, Kate, Bill, and Vanessa, Nancy and George went to their room to tally up all the accounts.

"There aren't any apparent inconsistencies," Nancy said, rifling through her notes. "At least, nobody contradicted anybody else about the times they were together. But we're not much further along. Everybody's covered for some of the crucial period—from twelve to five—but nobody's covered for all of it."

"Except for Bill Denton," George said, sitting on the end of her bed. "Remember? He was on the phone in his room from noon until one, when Coining walked him to his car. Then he left for Chicago and didn't return until about five."

"We don't *know* he was on the phone for that hour," Nancy said. "I remember the name of the guy he was supposedly talking to. Leo Mallet, in Chicago. Let's see if we can track him down and check out Bill's story."

There was a cordless phone on the night table between the two beds. Taking the handset to the table near the window, Nancy started calling. After a half hour's work, she turned off the phone and set it down.

"So much for that," she reported. "Leo Mallet is a mystery writer, a client of Bill's. He just confirmed that they were on the phone together from noon until about one. Bill told him he was going to drive into the city, partly because he couldn't think straight with all the construction noise outside his window. Mallet said that during some of the call, the noise was so bad that he could barely hear Bill. Bill showed up at Mallet's apartment later in the afternoon. By the way, Mallet confirmed that Bill's agency is not in good financial shape."

"He probably spent all his profits on that fancy sports car," George joked. "What about the phone company?"

Nancy shrugged. "I asked the operator to check for time and charges. There was a call to Mallet's number yesterday at eleven fifty-eight. It lasted sixty-two minutes. What do you want to bet that Bill was planning to let the foundation pay for it?"

George laughed, then quickly she became somber again. "So, we're back where we started," she said. "You and I weren't here. Neither was Vanessa or Erika as far as we know, and Bill was gone. That leaves Patrick, Kate, Julian, and Professor Coining. Any of them could have sneaked into the study and stolen the figurines."

"If he or she knew how to get into the safe," Nancy pointed out. "That's no problem for Kate, she knows the combination. She could have been waiting to take the figurines until there were suspects around. But who else?"

"What about Erika?" George suggested.

Nancy nodded thoughtfully. "She did tell me she spent time here when Dorothea was alive. What if she sneaked onto the grounds *before* the time she said she got here? She could have used a secret passage to get into the house and take the jeweled figures. All she'd need was the combination to the safe."

George shook her head. "We're not getting anywhere, Nan. Why don't you call Chief McGinnis, and ask him to see if any of these people has a criminal record? You never know— one of them might be a safecracker!"

"Can't hurt to try." Nancy picked up the phone again and punched in the River Heights Police Department number. It took her a while to convince Chief McGinnis that it was urgent, but he finally agreed. Nancy sat with the handset on her lap, tapping her fingers on the table, until he came back on the line.

"Thanks, Chief," she said a few moments later.

"Well?" George asked. "Does one of the guests have a criminal record?"

Nancy nodded excitedly. "One of them served time in prison a few years ago as part of a burglary gang. And guess what his special talent was—cracking safes!"

George's jaw dropped. "So we've found our crook! Who is it, Nan?"

"It's Julian. Julian Romarain, of Murder to Go!"

Chapter
Nine

GEORGE LOOKED flabbergasted. "Julian?" she said. "A safecracker?"

"An *ex*-safecracker, as far as we know," Nancy corrected. "But he apparently has the skills to have broken into Dorothea's safe and stolen the figurines."

"I noticed that there was something between him and Kate," George added. "I bet they planned the theft together, and that's why Kate didn't want to call the police last night."

Nancy frowned. "I noticed the connection between them, too, but why would Kate need to use a safecracker? She's the only one around who knows the combination to the safe."

"Oh—I forgot," George said. "Well, maybe

they're not in it together, but she figured out that he's the thief. If she's in love with him, she might try to shield him from the police."

"Even after he murdered Maxine?" Nancy asked. "*If* the two crimes are connected, that is."

Nancy got to her feet. "The only way we're going to straighten this out is to confront him— or her." She put the cordless phone back on its base and started for the door.

"Who do we talk to first?" George asked, as they headed down the hall.

"Whoever we find first," Nancy said.

Kate was in the study, sitting behind Dorothea's desk and making notes in the margin of a computer printout. The late-afternoon sun shone on her face, emphasizing the lines of tiredness and stress. She raised her head as Nancy and George came in.

"Can we talk for a minute or two?" Nancy asked.

Kate hesitated before answering. "I—will it take long? I've got a thousand details to take care of. Armand is coming down tonight with some important donors."

"Just a minute or two," Nancy repeated. She and George sat down in two chairs next to the desk. Taking a deep breath, Nancy got straight to the point. "How well do you know Julian?"

Kate stiffened. "Why do you ask?"

"Do you know about his personal history?" Nancy pressed.

"I know that he was once in trouble with the law, if that's what you mean," Kate said, her chin held high. "But he paid for his mistakes, and his past is nobody's concern but his."

Clearing her throat, George said, "You did ask Nancy to investigate the theft of those jeweled figures. If one of the suspects is a convicted safecracker, I think that his past becomes her business."

Kate's face was still, almost expressionless. Then unexpectedly she dropped her head into her hands and began to sob. Nancy and George sat in an uncomfortable silence and waited for the storm to pass.

Finally Kate took a deep breath, wiped her eyes, and said, "I'm sorry. It's just that I've been dreading this moment since last night when we discovered the gold figurines weren't in their case. I knew Julian's record would come up sooner or later. And I knew that the moment it did, he'd be accused of the theft."

"Are you and Julian, er, close?" asked George.

Kate sighed. "Not nearly as close as I'd like," she replied. "I know he cares about me, but he's always brooding about his past. He told me we can't get involved because it might ruin my reputation. It's so ridiculous! Okay, he made a mistake, a bad one. But he's put that behind him.

He started his own business, and it's totally legal. Who cares what happened years ago?"

Nancy couldn't help feeling sorry for Kate. "How did you two meet?" she asked.

A smile crossed Kate's face. "Dorothea was one of the first experts Julian talked into coming to one of his Mystery Weekends. We went to this creaky, spooky, old resort hotel. Dorothea loved every minute."

"Did Dorothea know about his past?" George asked.

Kate scowled at her. "You can't leave it alone, can you?" she demanded. "As a matter of fact, she did. Julian told her. And she was fascinated. She asked him to come here one weekend and give her a lecture-demonstration on how a professional opens a safe. She went on to write a wonderful safecracking scene in her next book."

"I read that!" George exclaimed. "It was in *The Golden Circle.*"

Nancy gestured with her head to the cabinet that concealed the safe. "Is that the safe he gave her the demonstration on?"

Kate's face hardened again. "Yes," she replied. "He managed to get it open in under five minutes. But I'm telling you, Julian did not steal those figurines. And neither did I. If chasing after us is your idea of conducting an investigation, I'm sorry I asked you to help."

"You wouldn't have thought we were very good

detectives if we'd ignored a possible lead like this, would you?" George asked.

"I guess not," Kate admitted reluctantly.

"I have to warn you," Nancy added. "By now Lieutenant Kitridge must know about Julian's record, too."

"Lieutenant Kitridge?" she asked in a shaky voice. "But he's working on Maxine's murder. He's already solved it. Erika killed her."

"She was just taken in for questioning. She hasn't been arrested, as far as I know," Nancy pointed out.

"If only Julian would trust me!" Kate burst out. "I know I could help him prove his innocence. But he won't talk to me at all."

Nancy thought George was thinking the same thing she was. Maybe the reason Julian wouldn't talk to Kate was that he didn't want her to know he was still a crook.

With a groan, Kate went on, "How am I supposed to think about throwing a party at a time like this?"

"Party?" George said, her eyes lighting up with interest.

"This evening, after dinner," Kate explained. "The mystery costume party. It was supposed to be one of the big events of the conference. Didn't you see it on the schedule?"

"Sure," Nancy said. "But I thought the whole conference was postponed."

"It was. But we've got tons of extra people coming to the party," Kate said. "The United Mystery Fans from Caldwell College are all coming in costume. We even hired a rock band called the Skeletons. I wanted to cancel, after everything that's happened. But Armand said we had to go ahead. He's bringing some major donors down from Chicago for it."

Picking up her pencil, she added, "I'm sorry to be rude, but I have to get back to work. Maybe it'll take my mind off my real problems—like what's going on with Julian."

The costume party took place in the ballroom of Mystery Mansion, an enormous space that took up one entire end of the west wing. Crystal chandeliers sparkled, and tall glass doors led out onto a terrace where Chinese lanterns flickered.

George adjusted her trench coat and fedora hat. "Do you think anyone will know I'm supposed to be Sam Spade?" she asked.

"Definitely. And I'm sure they'll know who I am," Nancy said, adjusting her cape and deerstalker hat. She'd already spotted two other Sherlock Holmeses, but still felt her choice was right for her.

Nancy's foot started moving to the beat as the band, all dressed in skeleton costumes, began playing a song with a driving beat. She was glad to see a lot of younger kids in costume—obviously they were from Caldwell College.

A dark-haired guy dressed as a Keystone Kop asked George to dance. As her friend moved onto the dance floor, Nancy heard someone calling her. "Nancy, I'd like you to meet Armand Wasserman, the president of the Burden Foundation," Kate said as she and Armand joined Nancy.

"I've heard a lot about you, Nancy," Mr. Wasserman said. "Kate tells me you're trying to get to the bottom of the—the awful things that have happened here."

"I just hope I can solve the mysteries," Nancy said truthfully.

Kate and the foundation president moved over to a group of conservatively dressed people. Nancy guessed they were the donors Kate had mentioned.

"Ah—Holmes! You're just the one I've been searching for."

Nancy turned to the stranger and laughed. She was peering at a mirror image of herself, except the other Holmes costume was worn by a cute blond guy. He asked her to dance. On the dance floor she saw that most of the other Mystery Mansion guests were also dancing. Professor Coining, dressed as the famous mystery author Ellery Queen, was spinning Vanessa around. The party was definitely easing the tension that had been caused by Maxine's murder and the theft of the figurines.

After half a dozen dances, Nancy excused herself and went to the refreshment table to get something to drink. George was there with Patrick, who looked like a 1930s gangster, in his double-breasted pinstripe suit and white spats.

"No, we're not really satisfied," Nancy heard George say as she came up. "Nancy called the police before we came down to the party, and they said they're just holding Erika overnight for questioning—not officially charging her."

Nancy was about to caution George not to talk about an ongoing investigation, when someone spoke up behind her.

"Anybody need anything from town tomorrow morning?" Bill Denton asked. "I'm going to go in first thing for the Sunday papers. I want to see what kind of coverage our mystery is getting."

"No, thanks," Patrick said coolly. George and Nancy shook their heads. As Bill walked away, Patrick added, "He probably hopes the publicity will make more people buy Aunt Dotty's books. I wonder if he ever thinks about anything besides his ten percent?"

Before Nancy could comment, Professor Coining came over to them, his brow beaded with perspiration. "Which one of you two ladies would like to dance?" he asked expectantly.

"No, really, I—" Nancy began as she was led out onto the dance floor.

The next half hour was a dizzying succession of twists and twirls. Nancy had to admit it was kind of fun, though, and the professor was a great dancer.

During a complex maneuver that involved having her arms wrapped around her in two different directions, she noticed Julian slipping out one of the french doors to a terrace at the front of the house.

What's he up to? she wondered.

It took her a few moments to excuse herself from the professor, but finally she was able to grab a flashlight from her purse and hurry out to the terrace. Peering past the long facade beyond the construction, Nancy saw what might have been Julian entering the summerhouse.

She hurried across the lawn. As she neared the summerhouse, she began to move silently. She crept up to one of the windows, cautiously boosting herself up to peek inside.

"What?" she said to herself, blinking. The summerhouse was empty!

Nancy sprang to the door and opened it. A Chinese lantern outside the door cast fantastic shadows over the table and the built-in benches that lined the walls inside. There was no place to hide, unless—

Nancy tugged at the seat of the nearest bench.

It swung up to reveal a croquet set. Under the others she found badminton rackets, a wicker picnic basket, a deflated soccer ball, a beach umbrella, and two glow-in-the-dark Frisbees.

Only one bench refused to open. She studied it, then felt along the underside. Nancy became excited as her fingers touched a button. When she pressed it, the seat released and sprang up. She found herself staring down a dark shaft with rungs set into a stone wall.

"So *this* is where Julian disappeared to," she murmured to herself.

She switched on her flashlight and swung herself over the side of the bench to scramble down the ladder. She counted the rungs as she went. At twenty, her feet touched rough pavement.

Somewhere up ahead, footsteps echoed. Pointing the tiny beam into the blackness, Nancy hurried along a damp, brick-walled tunnel that curved and dipped confusingly. Other tunnels branched off on either side—or was she now following one of the branches? She wasn't certain anymore.

Stopping and listening intently, she no longer heard the footsteps ahead of her. It seemed impossible, but they were *behind* her now. Nancy felt the hairs on the back of her neck stand up. Someone was following her!

A moment later her flashlight flickered once, then died. Oh, great, Nancy thought. She shut her eyes tightly, hoping that would help her to adapt more quickly to the darkness.

All at once she froze, hardly daring to breathe. Wasn't that the scrape of a shoe on pavement she heard, somewhere very near?

She licked her lips and called out, "Is somebody there? Who is it?" Her voice echoed in the darkness.

The only answer was a low, evil laugh.

Chapter

Ten

THE MAD LAUGHTER swelled and echoed, bouncing off the walls from what seemed like four directions at once.

Nancy's instincts took over. She ran, keeping her left hand lightly resting against the wall and her right arm stretched out in front of her. She only hoped there weren't any holes or staircases!

The tunnel twisted and turned, until she lost all sense of direction. She was panting loudly now, and the pounding of her shoes on the irregular pavement made it impossible to hear if her pursuer was gaining on her.

Soon Nancy began to sense, if not quite see, the shape of the passage ahead. It curved to the right and began to slant upward. Then, around the curve, there was light, streaming in from a side passage. Nancy ran along the new passage and saw a red door set into the side wall, a dozen feet away. The door was slightly ajar.

Nancy stopped, leaned against the wall, and tried to catch her breath. Then she concentrated on listening. From up ahead came a low hum, like the sound of many distant voices, and the rhythmic thump of an electric bass. From behind her there was only silence. Her pursuer must have given up the chase.

Creeping up to the door, Nancy peeked through the gap. On the other side was a small room she had never seen before. It was furnished with a metal desk and a row of gray metal file cabinets. The ceiling light was on, but the room was empty. Nancy pushed the door open and stepped through. When she closed the door behind her, she saw that it wasn't a door but a bookcase. Only someone who was looking for it would have noticed that one of the middle shelves could be pushed in half an inch to release the latch on the concealed door.

Nancy went to the door of the room and opened it into Dorothea's study. Nancy hurried across the darkened room and through that door to the hall. She was eager to reach the ballroom to see who was there and, more importantly, who wasn't.

Back in the ballroom, the lights were down and the Skeletons were playing a slow number. The lead singer was swaying at the microphone with his eyes closed. Seeing couples dancing close made Nancy wish that Ned Nickerson, her steady boyfriend, were here. She'd give anything to be dancing with him right now.

Come on, Drew. You've got a mystery to solve, she thought, mentally shaking herself. She carefully surveyed the room and spotted Julian near the windows, dancing with Kate. Bill was with a woman Nancy didn't recognize. Vanessa was on the sidelines, talking to Armand Wasserman. George was dancing with Professor Coining.

Where was Patrick? Then she saw him at the far end of the room, dancing with a college girl who had come dressed as Vampira.

Nancy frowned. There was nothing to tell her who the person down in the tunnel had been. The obvious suspect was Julian. Maybe he had noticed her following him, hidden in a side passage until she went by, and then come after her. It was certainly possible. Then again, she'd had a strong impression that Julian had been some distance in front of her when she first heard someone *behind* her.

Whoever it was had to know the tunnels and passages very well. He or she had managed to find the way back to the ballroom, in the dark, and get there while Nancy was still fumbling around in the maze of tunnels. Who knew the house that well?

Patrick, of course, had spent much of his childhood here. Kate had worked for Dorothea for years, then taken on the job of converting Mystery Mansion into a museum. Vanessa and Bill had both been close to the novelist—they had probably visited the house often.

Nancy's thoughts were interrupted as the Skeletons' lead singer announced that the band was taking a break. As everyone clapped, Nancy edged through the crowd to George's side.

"Where have you been?" George demanded. "Professor Coining was driving me nuts! He wouldn't let me stop dancing!"

Nancy glanced around. "Let's go over by the windows. It's less crowded there," she said. "I need to talk."

As soon as they were in a secluded spot, Nancy told George what had happened in the underground passages.

"That's awful!" George exclaimed, horrified. "Nancy, you could have been killed! Do you have any idea who it was?"

Nancy shook her head. "I was hoping you could help me figure it out. Did you see anyone leave the party?"

"I can tell you for sure that Professor Coining

didn't leave the party," George replied, rolling her eyes. "The way he kept spinning me around, I could barely keep track of where *I* was, much less anybody else."

"Well, whoever it was obviously wanted to scare me off," Nancy said. "Everybody who's staying here this weekend heard Kate ask us to find the person who stole the gold figurines. The question is, was the person trying to scare me off the case in general, or specifically trying to scare me away from exploring the secret passages?"

"You mean, you think the figures might be hidden somewhere in the passages?" George asked.

"I wish I knew," Nancy said. She didn't bother to hide her frustration. "They could be anywhere —the passages, the summerhouse, the rose garden, the maze. . . . This place was *made* for hiding things."

When George didn't say anything, Nancy looked at her. "Earth to George," she said, waving her hands in front of George's eyes. George just stared straight ahead.

"The golden antelope," she murmured. "It's just possible. . . . Why didn't I think of it before?"

"Think of what?" Nancy asked.

"Is there a maze somewhere near the house?" George asked. Nancy told her about the maze of hedges she'd seen that morning. "We've got to check it out first thing tomorrow!" George exclaimed.

Nancy planted her hands on her hips. "George, will you please tell me what you're talking about?"

"The Golden Antelope," George repeated. "It's one of Dorothea Burden's best novels, all about the theft of this really valuable gold statue, and a lot of crooks come to search for it."

"I think I saw the movie," Nancy said.

George nodded distractedly. "The point is, the golden antelope was hidden in a secret compartment at the base of a statue of Mercury, at the center of the maze. Did you know that Mercury was the god of thieves?"

"I didn't even know there was one, but I see what you're getting at," said Nancy. "If our thief is following Dorothea's book, then we should find the figurines in that maze. George, you're brilliant!"

George's cheeks reddened. "Even if we do recover them, we still won't know who stole them."

She fell silent as Kate walked up to join them.

"I spoke to Julian," Kate said with a touch of defiance in her voice. "I told him that you'd found out about him. He said it didn't matter. He swore he had nothing to do with stealing those figurines, and I believe him. I don't care whether you do or not." Before Nancy or George could say a word, Kate took off.

George focused on Kate until she was out of sight. "I don't know, Nan. I think she's telling the truth."

"Maybe," Nancy said, "but we can't rule out any suspect at this point."

Clapping rose up from the crowd as the Skeletons returned to the stage, picked up their instruments, and launched into a fast song. George began tapping her foot, but Nancy was too preoccupied with the case to think about dancing.

"You know, I'd like to take a look at *The Golden Antelope*," she told George. "There's bound to be one around somewhere."

"There's probably a copy in the library," George suggested. "Anyway, here comes Professor Coining. Let's get out of here!"

The lighting in the library was so dim that Nancy could hardly read the lettering on the backs of the rows of books. She didn't want to turn on more lights and alert anyone to their presence. She pulled down a book at random and opened it. The title page, in old-fashioned type, said the book was "A true and faithful narrative of the dreadful murther of Sir Edmund Bury Godfrey." The date at the bottom was 1679.

"This place is awesome," Nancy told George,

carefully replacing the antique book on the shelf. "I'd like to spend a few weeks in here!"

"I don't see any of Dorothea's books," George reported. "They're probably kept somewhere else."

Nancy suddenly snapped her fingers, recalling the bookcase that masked the secret doorway in the little file room off Dorothea's study. "Of course!" she said. "I know where they are. Come on."

Nancy led the way out of the library and down the hall toward Dorothea's study. As they drew near, she stopped suddenly and put her fingers to her lips. The study door was slightly ajar, and a ray of light shone around it. Nancy was sure that the room had been dark before. And hadn't she shut the door behind her? Someone was in there!

Moving as silently as they could, the two girls crept up to the door and peered around its edge. Next to Nancy, George stifled a gasp.

Professor Coining was kneeling in front of Dorothea's safe! He had a scrap of paper in his left hand. With his right he was slowly turning the combination dial, first to the left, then to the right. He paused, then gave the chrome handle a hard twist and pulled. The safe door swung open.

George made a small movement, brushing her trench coat against the wood of the door. The noise was very faint, but the professor obviously heard it. He spun around and stared in the direction of the door. Nancy took an involuntary step backward.

Professor Coining listened intently for another moment. Then he thrust his right hand into the pocket of his jacket and started across the room, straight toward Nancy and George!

Chapter

Eleven

"LOOK OUT! He's got a weapon!" Nancy gasped. She pushed George back from the study door with her elbow.

The door swung open, and Professor Coining seemed to fill the opening. His eyes widened as he recognized Nancy and George. Then an expression of relief came over his face. He took his hand from inside his coat pocket and let it fall to his side.

"Ah, my favorite dancing partners," he said. "What brings you two here?"

"We saw you in Dorothea's study just now," Nancy said. "We saw you open her safe."

Cautiously he replied, "Oh?"

"We both saw you," George said. "How did you know the combination?"

101

"Oh, that," he said dismissively. "Shall we go inside? I hate carrying on an important conversation in a public corridor."

"All right," Nancy finally agreed.

The three of them went into the study, and the professor closed the door behind them. He immediately began talking.

"I found the combination on this index card," he said, reaching into his pocket.

Nancy stiffened. "Not so fast," she said, grabbing his right wrist with both hands.

He slowly produced a three-by-five card and held it out to George. She glanced at it and said, "It looks like a safe combination, all right."

Nancy was still grasping the professor's wrist. "Now the weapon," she said. "Take it out slowly and drop it on the floor."

With a sigh, Professor Coining reached inside his jacket and took out a flimsy, plastic-handled paring knife. "I borrowed it from the kitchen," he explained as he let it fall to the ground. "With all the mayhem in this house, I felt I should be prepared to defend myself if necessary."

Nancy took the card from George. "Where did you find this?" she asked dubiously.

"In the most obvious place imaginable," Professor Coining told her. "It was taped to the underside of one of Dorothea's desk drawers. Anybody who has read as much sensational fiction as I have knows to search there first."

George was already halfway to the desk. "Which drawer?" she asked.

"The second one down on the right."

George pulled out the drawer and peered at its underside. "Two strips of cellophane tape, about three inches apart," she reported. "He could be telling the truth."

"Of course I am," he said indignantly. "May I go now?"

"Not yet," Nancy told him. "What were you looking for in the safe?"

Professor Coining grew suddenly uncomfortable. "Well, if you must know, I was looking for that wretched manuscript," he finally said. "The one Maxine told us about yesterday, before she was killed. Most of my book about Dorothea is already at the compositors, being set into type. I have to see this new manuscript, to make sure it doesn't contradict any of my important points about Dorothea and her work. If it does, and I let my book come out uncorrected, I'll be a laughingstock."

He seemed sincere, but Nancy was still suspicious. "What made you think you'd find it in the safe?" she asked. "Why not in Maxine's room? She had it last, didn't she?" Nancy had purposely not told the other guests about Erika's theft of the manuscript, so as far as Professor Coining knew, Maxine was the last to have it.

"I did look there," the professor admitted.

"Just before I came down to the party. It was simply a matter of breaking that ridiculous paper seal the police had put on the door. But the manuscript wasn't there. I searched carefully for it."

George nodded. "So when you didn't find it you figured that maybe she gave it back to Kate."

"That's right," Professor Coining said. "Maxine did promise to return it, and I thought Kate would put the manuscript in the safe. Is there anything else I can tell you? I'd like to get back to the party before the band calls it a night.

"What do you say, George," he added, wiggling his eyebrows up and down. "Shall we go cut a rug?"

"Oh, no! No, thank you," George said quickly. "I—I have a headache."

"So do I," Nancy said as the professor turned to ask her. She didn't even bother trying to sound convincing.

"It's your loss, ladies," he retorted, then headed for the door.

As soon as he was gone, Nancy went over to the safe and peered inside. No manuscript. Then, nudging the door shut with her knee, she turned to George and said, "Maybe he knew the combination to the safe all along. How do we know he didn't steal the figurines?"

George shrugged. "We don't, I guess. But it's pretty clear that he doesn't know about Erika taking that manuscript, which means he's not the one who took it from Erika's room."

"We're still not any closer to solving this case," Nancy pointed out. "But maybe there's a clue in that book you mentioned."

Hurrying to the small file room, she scanned the titles in the bookcase. *The Golden Antelope* was there, in five languages and in several editions. She pulled down a copy of the American paperback and put it in the pocket of her cape.

"Why don't we go back to the party now?" George suggested. "I was really having a lot of fun, until I got snared by the Dancing Professor!"

"Great idea," Nancy said.

As they went back down the hallway toward the ballroom, Nancy saw a familiar-looking figure walking ahead of them. Hearing their footsteps, he glanced over his shoulder, and Nancy recognized Julian's well-trimmed beard.

He spun around and angrily stalked toward them. "You've been following me!" he said. "Well, it had better stop, right now!"

"We weren't following you!" George declared indignantly. "We were just walking down the hall, minding our own business."

Julian ignored her, and continued to stare at Nancy. "Kate told me that you found out about me," he said. "That was a long time ago. I'm completely legit now. I don't care if you believe me or not, but stop trailing me!"

He pointed an accusing finger at Nancy. "Don't bother denying it. I saw you follow me outside before. And I heard you behind me in the tunnel."

Nancy couldn't believe he was admitting he'd been in the tunnel. "Now that you mention it, just what were you doing there?"

"Hunting for those stupid figurines, of course. I knew that the longer they were missing, the surer it was that someone was going to find out about—well, you know—and give me some major grief."

"Why the tunnels?" George asked. "This place is filled with other possible hiding places."

"I was up pretty early this morning," Julian replied. "I was looking out the window of my room when I saw Erika Olsen go into the summerhouse, with a big tote bag over her shoulder. From the way she kept glancing back behind her, I knew she was up to something. And, of course, I knew all about the hidden tunnel entrance in the summerhouse. So I figured she was probably taking the figures down there to hide them."

"Why her?" Nancy demanded. "She didn't even get to Mystery Mansion yesterday until after five o'clock. The figurines were probably stolen a little after noon."

Julian shrugged. "With all the commotion here yesterday, she could have sneaked onto the property. She had as good an opportunity to take the figures as anyone."

He had a point, Nancy realized. Still . . . "Without any corroboration, that story won't hold up," she told him.

"I'm not a detective," Julian said bitterly. "I'm just an innocent—repeat, innocent—bystander." With that, he stalked away.

"What do you think?" George finally asked.

"I don't know," Nancy confessed. "Erika *was* in that secret passage this morning to get to Maxine's room. So maybe she was around yesterday, too."

"Maybe Maxine knew Erika stole the figurines and accused her. Maybe Erika did kill her," George said in a rush. "All that stuff about the manuscript could have just been a cover-up."

"I don't know," Nancy said slowly. "The manuscript *is* missing." She shook her head in frustration. "Come on. Let's head back to the party. Maybe some dancing will help clear our heads."

Nancy was running through a constantly changing maze of tunnels. She didn't dare look behind her. Something she couldn't name was close behind, and gaining on her. Suddenly the tunnel ahead ended abruptly at a heavy iron door. She tugged at the handle, but it didn't move. Desperately she pressed the pearl button to the right of the door. A buzzer sounded, impossibly far away, but no one came. She pressed again. The buzzer was louder this time, as if it were right next to her ear. . . .

Nancy forced her eyes open and groped for the phone on the bedside table. "Hello?" she mumbled into it.

"Hi, Nancy. I didn't wake you, did I?"

Nancy smiled sleepily as she recognized Ned's deep voice. "What time is it?"

"It's after eight. I wanted to catch you before you went off to some mystery lecture. How's the conference going?"

Nancy sat up, pushed the pillow behind her back, and switched the cordless phone to her other hand. "So far we've got one murder, one case of safecracking, and one other important theft," she reported.

After a short silence, Ned asked, "You mean, you've been discussing classic crimes?"

"No, we've got some real ones." She quickly filled him in on what had been going on.

"Wow," Ned said. "Well, listen, Nan, if you're on a case, maybe I should let you go."

"I've always got time for you, Nickerson," Nancy said quickly. "So how's everything at Emerson?"

They talked for about five minutes. When George showed signs of waking up, Nancy told Ned, "I'd better go. I miss you."

"I miss you, too," Ned said. "Take care of yourself, okay?"

"Don't worry, I always do. 'Bye." She blew a kiss into the handset before turning it off.

"Who was that?" George's sleepy voice asked from the other bed.

Nancy didn't answer. She was staring down at the cordless phone in her hand. A wild idea was tickling the edges of her mind.

"George!" she exclaimed.

George propped herself up on one elbow and rubbed her eyes. "What is it?" she asked.

"I think I know who stole the figurines!"

Chapter

Twelve

W**HERE ARE WE GOING?**" George asked, still half asleep as she followed Nancy down Mystery Mansion's main staircase.

The two girls had dressed in record time, throwing on jeans and long-sleeved shirts.

"I'll explain in a minute," Nancy replied.

She hurried down the hallway to Dorothea's study and tried the knob. It was unlocked, just as it had been the night before. Pushing it open, she told George, "Wait for me here. I won't be long."

Nancy didn't take the time to explain and took off at a run, returning to the second floor.

Bill Denton's door was three down from the landing, in the opposite direction from Nancy and George's room. Nancy tapped softly on it and waited. No answer. She knocked more vigorously, but there still was no response. Good, she thought. He must have gone into town for the Sunday papers, the way he said he was going to. She tried the knob—the door was locked.

It took her three minutes of work with her own bedroom key, nail file, and bent paper clip, but she finally got the door open. Slipping inside, she shut it behind her, then checked out the room. It contained two single beds, one of them still made up. The ornate furniture and heavy curtains were old-fashioned, although Nancy didn't recognize the particular mystery genre they represented. The most modern touch was the cordless phone on the table between the beds.

Nancy went straight to the closet and began turning the coat hooks. On the fourth try, a hook moved and the secret panel opened. Clutching her flashlight, she stepped into the passage. The door closed behind her.

A flight of concrete steps led down to a narrow passage, with tunnels leading off it. Nancy tried to visualize the layout of the rooms and halls on the ground floor, then chose one of the passages. Soon after, she let out a soft whoop of triumph. Directly in front of her was the red door. She worked the latch and pushed. On the other side was the small office and file room that adjoined the study.

Hurrying across to the study door, she opened it and said, "Peek-a-boo!"

George had been standing by a table, leafing through a magazine. Now she dropped the magazine, and whirled around. "How did you get there?"

Nancy showed George the bookcase hiding the door to the network of secret passages. "There's a passage that leads from Bill Denton's room right here, which happens to be near the safe."

George's mouth fell open. "You mean you think he stole the figurines? But how——"

Nancy held up a hand. "I have to check something out with Kate before I can be positive," she said. "Come on!"

They found Kate in the dining room, eating a breakfast of dry toast and tea. In response to Nancy's questions, she told them that Bill had been given a room away from the construction noise, but he had gone to Kate and asked to be moved to a room where he had often stayed when Dorothea was still alive. He said he felt sentimental about it.

"Do you happen to have the home number of the construction-crew foreman?" Nancy asked.

"I should have it somewhere," Kate answered. She left the table, returning a few minutes later with a slip of paper. "Good luck," she said as she handed it to Nancy. "It's the weekend, you know. He may have gone fishing or something. But that's what you're doing, too, isn't it?"

"Not really," Nancy replied. "Fishermen throw out their bait and wait to see what bites. It's different for me. I have a very good idea of what I'm going to catch."

Once she and George were back in their room, Nancy dialed the number Kate had given her. The call was answered on the third ring. She spoke for a few minutes, then put the handset back on the base.

"Now will you tell me what this is all about?" George asked, sitting on Nancy's bed.

Nancy grinned. "Sure. Remember Bill's alibi? He said he was on the phone from about noon to one. And Mallet, the guy he was talking to then, noticed how noisy the call was. Bill said it was because of the construction going on outside his window."

"But Bill chose that room," George protested. "He must have known it was going to be noisy."

"Oh, he knew, all right," Nancy said. "Except for a very minor detail. On Friday, the construction crew took its lunch hour from noon to one. And that was exactly when Bill was on the phone with his client."

"Wait a minute, didn't you just say they were on their lunch hour?" George asked, holding up her hands. "There wouldn't have been any noise then."

"Exactly," Nancy said triumphantly. "Bill

113

knew that Kate was going to be away from the study, meeting with Julian and Patrick, from noon to one. So at noon, he placed a call to his chattiest client, on the *cordless* phone in his room. Then he went through the hidden passage to the study, opened the safe, took the figurines, and returned the way he had come, *carrying the phone with him the whole time.* That's why the phone call was noisy—the farther he got from the phone base, the more static there was. And he explained it to his friend as construction noise."

"Nancy, that's brilliant! Then he killed Maxine because she found out what he'd done and threatened to expose him."

"Maybe," Nancy said. "But I think he had another motive, too. There was that phone call with Dorothea that Maxine had taped—Maxine hinted that the call indicated that Bill had been embezzling money from Dorothea. I bet that a careful check of the books from Bill's literary agency will show that he's not only broke, he's a crook as well."

George's face fell. "But we don't have a single bit of evidence against him," she pointed out.

"Maybe not, but I know where we might be able to find some," Nancy said, grinning at George.

A gleam of understanding shone in George's

dark eyes. "Of course! Mercury, the god of thieves!"

Nancy and George sat in the sun room, where they could keep a close eye on the parking lot. It seemed like forever before Bill's sports car returned. Bill climbed out and started toward the house, a stack of newspapers under his arm.

"Now!" Nancy muttered. "While there's no chance that he'll see us."

She and George went outside and around to the side of the house. Less than a minute later they were slipping through the entrance to the maze. Hidden within the tall, overgrown hedges, Nancy was sure no one could see them now.

"Look," she said, pointing toward the hedge along one side of the maze. "Those twigs are broken, but the leaves on them are still green."

"Hey, what's this?" George asked. She plucked a bit of white wool from a bush and showed it to Nancy. "I bet it came from his cable-knit sweater," Nancy said excitedly. "He must have come through here. Now, how do we get to the center?"

The maze was a confusing collection of wrong turns and dead ends. The girls had to retrace their steps and try other routes a half-dozen times. Finally they reached a grassy circle about ten feet across. In the center, on a waist-high stone pedestal, was a bronze statue of a man poised on the ball of one foot. Little wings grew from his heels.

"Mercury," George said. "Just like in the book."

"Do you remember where the secret compartment was or how to open it?" Nancy asked, stepping right up to the statue.

"Oh, sure. That was an awesome scene, when the heroine discovered the secret. She had to press down on one of the wings on Mercury's feet."

"Then let's see how closely Dorothea followed her own book," Nancy said.

She bent over to study the little wings on the right foot, which was resting on the pedestal. One of the wings was obviously cast as one piece with the foot, but the other . . .

Nancy didn't want to disturb any prints, so she pulled down her shirt sleeve to cover her hand, then gently turned the wing. It resisted at first, but then it moved and there was a muffled click. One of the facing stones on the pedestal slid outward a half inch.

"Nancy!" George exclaimed.

Nancy's pulse was racing as she grasped the edge of the stone and pulled it forward. Behind it was a compartment about a foot square, with a cardboard shoe box in its side. As delicately as she could, Nancy pulled the box toward her and lifted the lid a few inches.

The gleam of gold and sparkle of jewels were unmistakable. She and George gazed down at the precious figurines.

"Wow," George said. "They're incredible!"

Nancy didn't want to spoil any fingerprints by touching the figurines. Carefully she replaced the lid of the box and pushed the stone door closed on it.

"We'd better get on the phone to Lieutenant Kitridge," she added.

They slipped out of the maze unnoticed and returned to the house. While Nancy called the lieutenant, George sat by a window in the living room with a view of the maze entrance. "Nobody's gone near it," she reported when Nancy returned.

"Good," Nancy said. "The lieutenant promised to have his men in concealed positions in half an hour. We should take turns getting some breakfast. You know the old saying—never trap a crook on an empty stomach!"

Thirty minutes later, Nancy and George found Bill Denton in the sun room, browsing through his newspapers. The girls pulled a couple of wicker chairs next to a window and sat down with the backs to him. They had brought two mugs of tea with them, which they drank while they talked.

"I wish someone would put together a guide to

Mystery Mansion," Nancy remarked, just loud enough for Bill to hear. "Dorothea built so many interesting features into it. Do you suppose they all came from her books?"

"I know that secret door in our closet did," George replied. "And some of the other features seem familiar, too. Did you read *The Golden Antelope?*"

"No, I missed that one. Why?"

George gave a little laugh that almost betrayed her nervousness. "Did you notice that overgrown maze at the side of the house? There was one like it in *The Golden Antelope*. It had a statue in the middle, with a secret compartment in the base."

"Really?" Nancy said, trying to sound very eager. "Hey, why don't we go check out the maze to see if it has a statue?"

"Okay," George replied. "But let's finish our tea first."

Behind them, Bill stood up, collected his newspapers, and walked away.

Nancy exchanged a grin with George. They waited in the sun room a few minutes longer, then returned to the living room to a window that had a view of the maze.

"Do you think he really took the bait?" George asked in an undertone.

"We'll know pretty soon," Nancy replied. Then she pointed and said, "Look, there he is!"

Bill was strolling casually across the lawn. It looked as if his path just happened to bring him close to the maze. He glanced at the entrance, then, as if on impulse, went inside.

Nancy took a deep breath, then another. The next thing she knew, a knot of people came boiling out of the maze entrance. Two of them, in blue uniforms, were trying to subdue Bill, who was struggling with them. Behind him, Lieutenant Kitridge was carefully holding a shoe box in both hands.

"They got him!" George exclaimed. She and Nancy ran outside just as the lieutenant finished informing Bill of his rights. When he saw the two teens, a flash of understanding crossed Bill's face.

"You've got it all wrong, Lieutenant," Bill said. "I didn't steal the figurines. I found them. I went looking for them inside the maze because of something in one of Dorothea's books. I was going to turn them over to you right away."

For a moment doubt welled up in Nancy's mind. Could Bill be telling the truth? But what about the strands of wool on the twigs of the maze? She looked at the box in Lieutenant Kitridge's hands, then glanced down at Bill's running shoes.

Taking a chance, Nancy said, "Maybe you can explain how the stolen figurines came to be in

119

your shoe box. Same brand, same color, and I'm willing to bet they're the same size, too."

Bill turned pale, and Nancy knew she'd guessed correctly.

"Come with me," Lieutenant Kitridge told Bill. "You can do the rest of your talking at headquarters."

Chapter

Thirteen

I CAN'T BELIEVE it was Bill," Vanessa said a half hour later.

Word of Bill's arrest and the recovery of the figurines had spread quickly. The police had just left with him in custody, and now everyone was gathered in the living room to hear all the details.

"I'm mortified that I didn't think of the statue of Mercury in the maze myself," said Professor Coining, who was leaning against the mantel, sipping a glass of mineral water. "And I confess I'm astonished that Bill relied on such a hopelessly obvious hiding place."

"It wasn't obvious until George and Nancy found it," Julian pointed out from the couch. He was openly relieved not to be a suspect anymore.

Vanessa nodded her agreement. "The way you

two lured Bill into incriminating himself was a masterstroke."

"Thanks," Nancy said, feeling her cheeks grow warm. In the chair next to hers, George's cheeks were also bright red. She seemed awed by the praise they had received from the mystery experts.

"I wonder what Bill intended to do with the figurines," Patrick said, sitting on the arm of George's chair.

"I can answer that," Kate said. She put down the tray of soft drinks she'd been passing around and reached into her sweater pocket. "I found this on my desk this morning." She passed a folded sheet of paper to Nancy.

Opening it, Nancy read aloud: " 'You can have the jeweled statues back for two hundred thousand dollars in used tens and twenties. You'll get delivery instructions by phone on Monday. Don't tell the cops or I'll melt down the statues. Signed, Berringer.' "

Professor Coining gave an amused snort. "That's the name of the brilliant jewel thief in Dorothea's book *Monte Carlo Carnival*. I'm afraid Bill had an exaggerated opinion of his talents."

"The worst thing is, we probably would have paid it," Kate said, shaking her head ruefully. "Now, thanks to Nancy and George, we won't have to."

"I'm not surprised that the thief turned out to be Bill," Julian said. Getting up from the couch, he walked over to the fireplace and stirred the coals with a poker. "I always thought there was something sleazy about him. But I have trouble imagining him as a killer."

"A killer?" Vanessa repeated, looking surprised. "Do you mean it was Bill, and not Erika, who killed Maxine? But why?"

Nancy told the others about the strange conversation she and George had overheard through the heating duct on Friday night and about the implied threat in Maxine's comment to Bill about a taped call from Dorothea. "She obviously knew that he had been stealing from Dorothea," Nancy concluded. "Maybe she also guessed that he had stolen the figurines. That meant she was a terrible danger to him, so he got rid of her. I imagine he found Erika's scarf somewhere and used it to frame her."

Professor Coining cleared his throat. "No, no," he said, shaking his head. "That can't possibly be right."

"What!" Patrick exclaimed. "What are you saying?"

"Am I correct in saying that Maxine was murdered not long before breakfast yesterday?" the professor continued, addressing Nancy.

"That's right," Nancy confirmed. "Sometime around eight o'clock."

"Then Bill Denton did *not* kill her. I can give him an ironclad alibi."

The room seemed to explode as everybody started talking at once. Nancy was just as shocked as the others. She waited for the hubbub to die down, then said, "I'd like to hear about it, Professor."

"Well, I am a bit of an insomniac, and yesterday morning I awoke at four or so and could not get back to sleep," he began. "Finally, at around five-thirty, I came downstairs to get a glass of milk. In the kitchen I found Bill, making himself a sandwich."

"I wondered who'd made that mess in the kitchen," Kate murmured.

"He seemed preoccupied," the professor continued. "I guessed that he needed something to distract him, and so, I confess, did I. I proposed a few hands of gin rummy. We returned to my room, where we chatted and played cards until after eight-thirty, when we came down together to breakfast."

"Let me get this straight," Nancy said. "Are you telling us that you and Bill were together every single moment from about five-thirty until after eight-thirty?"

"That's correct," Professor Coining replied with an emphatic nod. "He could not possibly have murdered Maxine Treitler."

Nancy felt her heart sink. Maxine's murderer

was still at large—and probably in that very room.

In her mind she tried to put the pieces of the puzzle together with what she knew. If Bill didn't kill Maxine, then the murder—and possibly the threat she and George had overheard—wasn't at all connected to the theft.

George interrupted Nancy's thoughts after a few minutes. Looking up, Nancy saw that Patrick was standing with her. "We'd like to go play a few games of tennis. We'll be back right after to help solve this case. Is that okay?"

Nancy didn't see any point in both of them being indoors and stewing. "Go on ahead," she told George. "I'll see you later."

Turning her mind back to Maxine's murder, Nancy thought of the scarf and the shoe print in the secret passageway. The police had tied both to Erika, so why did Nancy doubt Erika was the killer?

Nancy thrummed her fingers on the chair arm. If only she had more to go on!

On an impulse, she jumped to her feet. Making an excuse to the others, she left the living room and went up to her room. She grabbed a flashlight and went into the closet to the secret door. If Erika had gotten to Maxine's room through the passages, then so could she. Maybe she had missed some important evidence.

The room that Maxine had occupied was four rooms down, on the opposite side of the hall. The passage from Nancy's room led down a steep flight of stairs, then up another and along a narrow hall. Nancy's first try brought her out in a closet with two tweed jackets. It was obviously Professor Coining's room. Closing the secret panel, she tried again.

Nancy was approaching the second door when her flashlight beam fell on a folded sheet of paper on the floor. Was this something Lieutenant Kitridge's officers had missed? Perhaps they hadn't ventured this far into the secret corridors.

She picked it up and held it in the beam of her flashlight. It was a note, with Dorothea Burden's name printed at the top.

I am speaking to you from beyond the grave. I cannot bear to share what I know with anyone while I am alive, but I don't dare let this knowledge die with me. This "novel" will tell you, and many others, the terrible truth that I have discovered. No one else knows what it contains. Kate does not even know it exists. I sent my dictation tapes secretly to a typing service in another city, and you are holding the only copy of the manuscript. Read it, then decide what you must do with it.

Dorothea Burden

Nancy stared blindly at the note. Dorothea's manuscript had revealed a "terrible truth" of some sort. Maxine had read it and died. Was it because she had learned that terrible truth? What kind of secret would inspire murder?

The answer had to be in the manuscript, Nancy realized—and the manuscript was missing.

Nancy leaned against a beam, trying to piece together all she knew about the book. Erika had admitted taking it from Maxine's room. Then, according to her, it had vanished from her room. Nancy had no way of being sure Erika was telling the truth. Without seeing the manuscript, she had no way of knowing if it implicated Erika—or someone else—in a crime.

As Nancy read through the letter again, she was struck by a sentence. Dorothea had recorded the text of the book, then had a typing service transcribe the tapes. What if the tapes were still around somewhere?

Her pulse racing, Nancy hurried back to her room. She grabbed her shoulder bag and put the flashlight in it. Seeing George's portable cassette player on the dresser, she took that, too. If she found Dorothea's tapes, she wanted to be prepared.

Nancy looked for and found Kate in the dining room, overseeing the setup for the buffet lunch. "I hope we can manage to reschedule the conference," she told Nancy. "Maybe for next month sometime. But I don't know. After all that's happened, people probably think that Mystery Mansion is jinxed."

"That'll just add to its charm," Nancy assured her. Turning the conversation to Dorothea Burden's books, she asked, "How did Dorothea work? Did she write the books out herself, or dictate them to you, or what?"

"When I first came to work for her, she typed everything herself, then revised it in pencil and gave me the corrected sheets to retype," Kate replied. "Sometimes we went through three or four drafts that way. But after her husband died and she became ill, she didn't have the strength to keep that up. Her last two books were dictated into a tape recorder."

"Really?" Nancy said. "Did you save the tapes? That might be an interesting feature for the museum, a chance to hear Dorothea reading—I mean, writing—her work."

"Good idea," Kate said, nodding thoughtfully. "I've got an entire file drawer stacked with cassettes. I've been meaning to go through and catalog them, but I haven't had a chance yet. Would you like to listen to one?"

Nancy tried to hide her excitement. "Why, yes, if it's no trouble."

"Not at all," Kate told her. "You know the

little file room off Dorothea's study? Look in the top drawer of the right-hand file cabinet. There's a tape player on the desk. Please be careful. Those tapes are irreplaceable."

"I will," Nancy promised.

Moments later she was looking in dismay at the dozens of tape cassettes in the file drawer. She picked up one and read the label: Memos, Letters Oct–Nov. Another said Notes for Memoirs. Still another was marked Danger Chaps 12–16.

Taking them out one by one, Nancy stacked the tapes on the top of the cabinet, ordering them as best she could. Some were labeled in ways she couldn't make out.

"Some of these aren't even labeled at all," Nancy muttered to herself. "This is hopeless!"

Then she noticed that several tapes were marked CH1, CH2, and so on. She had been reading CH as an abbreviation for chapter. But the title of the missing book was *The Crooked Heart*—CH! She grabbed the first of the marked tapes, inserted it into the player, and put on the headphones. Holding her breath, she pressed the Play button.

"The Crooked Heart, Chapter One. Why should he be rich, while I am poor?" said the voice of an elderly woman. "He is old and used up, but I have all of life before me. He is all that stands in my way. I would smash him with a hammer or throw him from a high window tomorrow, but then they would punish me. Punish me, for daring to claim what should be mine!

"But I am clever, sly, cunning. When I have carried out my plan, no one will know. No one will suspect. Why should they? An old man, an old *rich* man, dies a natural death. He leaves everything to his sick, dying wife, who has only one relative in the world. It happens every day. And it will happen again, very soon, in this house."

Nancy pushed the Stop button and stared down at the recorder. What was this about? A wealthy, old man and a young person who planned to kill him for his money. Maxine had said that the book was a fictionalized version of a real crime, Nancy recalled. But whose crime, and against whom?

Suddenly an image flashed in Nancy's mind of the portrait of Dorothea's husband in the living room. What was it that Vanessa had told her? That he had been in good shape, that no one had expected him to die as suddenly as he did. Yes, that was it. With him gone, there was only Dorothea, who was quite frail.

And Patrick.

That was it! Dorothea had somehow learned that her nephew, her only living relative, was responsible for the death of her husband. Perhaps she'd been unable to prove it, so she had found this way of punishing him for his crime—writing a book that everyone who knew him would understand.

Why hadn't she thought of Patrick before? In her mind, Nancy saw Patrick in his purple and green running suit gathering the scattered pages from the ground and handing them back to Erika. He must have recognized the book and then stolen it from Erika's room! By now he had probably destroyed it, not realizing that the book existed on tape as well.

Nancy stood up, gathered the *CH* cassettes, and hid them behind a row of Dorothea's books in the bookcase. She didn't dare risk taking them with her. Next she went to a window and looked out at the tennis court. Patrick and George were still engrossed in their game. She was afraid Patrick might suspect something if she interrupted them. There was no reason to think he'd hurt George, since he didn't realize Nancy was on to him.

Nancy hurried upstairs and set to work on the locked door of Patrick's room. After several minutes the lock clicked open, and she slipped inside.

The first thing she noticed was that the room smelled faintly of smoke. She crossed to the ornate fireplace and knelt down to examine the grate. It was clean—*too* clean. Someone had done a careful job of sweeping away every speck of ash from the fireplace. Nancy thought for a moment, then reached up and groped around inside the lowest part of the flue. As she had hoped, there was a smoke ledge, put there to stop smoke from blowing back into the room. And caught on the smoke ledge . . .

The blackened fragment of paper was no more than an inch across, but she could still make out the typed letters *ed Heart.*

"Crooked Heart!" Nancy crowed softly. Patrick must have burned the manuscript in this fireplace, then swept up the ashes. Nancy hoped that enough ashes remained for the forensic scientists to reconstruct parts of the manuscript. They would be swarming over this room as soon as she told Lieutenant Kitridge what she had learned.

Something warned her—a subtle change in the quality of the light or a faint sound—that someone was behind her. She started to whirl around, but before she could, an arm wrapped itself around her neck in a choke hold. The pressure on her carotid artery was agonizing.

Nancy tried desperately to free herself. She clawed and tore at the arm with both hands, but the pressure only grew stronger. A red haze spread in front of her eyes. Then the room went dark.

Chapter

Fourteen

NANCY'S THROAT ached horribly. Her left knee hurt, and something was digging into her back. She had a constant buzzing in her ears and a throbbing pain above each temple.

Nancy opened her eyes, then snapped them shut again. A bare bulb hung directly overhead, and the glare made the pain in her head a thousand times worse.

As she became more alert, she realized that her left leg was doubled under her—that was the reason her knee ached. She rolled to the right, onto her side, and straightened her leg.

Gradually the pain in her head subsided. Pushing herself up into a sitting position, Nancy opened her eyes and looked around.

She was on the floor of a steel cage whose bars rose to just beneath the low ceiling. The cage took up most of the space in a narrow, windowless room with a single steel door. Nancy shuddered at the updated version of a medieval dungeon. She didn't want to think about what Patrick planned for her. Even though he wasn't in the room now, Nancy was sure he'd return.

She got to her feet and examined her space more carefully. Aside from the cage, there was nothing in the room except a wooden folding chair. On the wall next to the door, just out of reach, were two electrical switches, one black and one bright red. The lock on the cage door was almost certainly pickproof.

Looking down, she saw that her shoulder bag was lying on the floor of the cage. That must have been what was digging into her back. She opened it, hoping to find something she could use to escape. There was only her heavy rubber flashlight and George's tape recorder.

Nancy's heart caught in her throat as a key scraped at the lock of the door. Whatever he planned to do with her, Nancy was determined to leave evidence behind. She thumbed the tiny volume wheel of the recorder to the maximum setting and pressed the red Record button. A second later, the door swung open.

"George!" Nancy called. A feeling of dread welled inside her as George stumbled forward, nearly falling. Patrick was right behind her, holding her arm in a hammerlock.

"Nancy? What—" George broke off as Patrick shoved the outer door closed with his foot and unlocked the cage. He pushed George inside.

"Welcome, ladies," he said, mocking them.

"What's going on?" George demanded. "Why did you bring us here? Unlock that door, Patrick!"

"Oh, I'm afraid I can't do that," he replied. "I'm not here at all, you see. Famed teen detective Nancy Drew and her faithful sidekick George Fayne went exploring the secret passages of Mystery Mansion on their own. They'd been warned that there were hidden dangers, but the daring sleuths didn't pay any attention. It's a sad story, but maybe it will keep others from making the same fatal mistake."

George ignored him as she spoke to Nancy. "Are you all right?"

Nancy nodded. George went on in a rush, "We were playing tennis, and the balls were dead, so he went up to his room to get a can of new ones. He was gone a long time, and when he came back, he said that you found something I had to come see right away. He took me down a hidden ladder in the summerhouse, into a tunnel. We walked for a while, then he suddenly twisted my arm, opened a door, and shoved me in here. What's going on?"

"He killed Maxine," Nancy replied. "When he found me in his room, he must have known I figured it out. He choked me until I passed out, then brought me down here. I guess he was afraid that you knew what I did, too."

"Please go on," Patrick said, sitting down on the folding chair and tilting it up on its back legs.

Anything to stall for time, Nancy thought. Aloud she said, "We made one big mistake. We thought that Maxine was killed to keep her from telling what she knew about the theft of the figurines." Nancy pitched her voice in the direction of the concealed tape recorder in her purse on the floor. "But what she discovered was a much more deadly secret. She found out that Patrick had murdered his uncle, and that Dorothea's last book, *The Crooked Heart,* was a detailed account of how he did it."

Patrick sprang to his feet. The chair teetered and fell over sideways. "How do you know that?" he demanded angrily. "I burned the only copy of that book!"

"I won't tell you how I know," Nancy said coolly. "And I won't tell you who else knows."

"You just signed your own death warrant," Patrick growled.

"So Patrick used Erika's scarf to frame her?" George asked, thinking out loud.

"I had to frame someone," Patrick said. "On Friday night Maxine told me about Aunt Dotty's book and strongly suggested that I leave the country. She made it clear that if I stayed, she'd make life hard for me."

So *that* was the conversation they'd heard through the vent, Nancy now knew.

"I had to silence her," Patrick continued, "but it had to be some way that couldn't be traced back to me. I didn't have enough time to hot-wire her shower."

"Is that how you murdered your uncle?" Nancy asked. "By electrocuting him in the shower?"

"Of course," Patrick replied. "It looked exactly like a heart attack. I still don't understand how Aunt Dotty caught on."

"It's just the sort of device a mystery writer like her would think of—the undetectable murder weapon," Nancy said.

"What about Maxine?" George insisted.

Patrick gave a self-satisfied smile. "I was lucky. There I was, jogging around the grounds, to give myself an alibi, and I ran straight into Erika. Everything in her bag went flying. And what do you suppose was in there?"

"The only copy of your aunt's book," said Nancy.

"Exactly. Well, I understood at once. Maxine would never have lent the manuscript to Erika, which meant Erika must have gone to Maxine's room and taken it. Her scarf had fallen out of her bag, too, and I tucked it under my jacket. Then I ducked into the passages, made my way to Maxine's room, and—"

He raised his two fists to throat level and pulled them apart sharply.

Nancy's stomach lurched. She'd faced dangerous criminals in the past, but she couldn't help being affected by Patrick's chilling, deadly tone.

"Then you must have gone to Erika's room, taken the manuscript, and destroyed it?" she asked. She had to keep him talking until she could figure a way out of there!

"Exactly," Patrick said proudly. "I didn't even stop to read it. It's a pity, in a way. I mean, how many people have been the main character of a book by a famous author?"

"Try Jack the Ripper," George said, shaking her head in disgust.

Patrick's nostrils widened with rage. He took a quick step toward the cage door, then seemed to think better of it. "There's no point in dragging this out," he said, his voice still calm. "Nobody's going to rescue you. Nobody even knows this room is here. The police will have to search a long time before they discover your tragic fate."

He broke into a laugh that jarred Nancy.

"That was you in the tunnel last night, wasn't it?" she demanded. "You followed me from the party to the summerhouse and down into the passages. Why?"

Patrick shrugged his shoulders. "Call it curiosity. I couldn't resist the chance to put a little scare into you. I enjoyed that."

"I bet you love pulling the wings off flies, too," George said. "I'm glad your aunt realized the kind of monster you are, in time to change her will."

For a brief moment Patrick's mask slipped again, showing the blind rage behind it.

"Oh, that!" he scoffed. "It's only money. And anyway, I'm working on a few ideas for recovering my rightful share. I wish you could be around to see how clever I am, but that's really not possible, I'm afraid."

Patrick took a step backward, toward the door of the little room. "From what I hear, you two have been in some tight spots together," he said. "But I guarantee that this one will be your last."

Laughing still, he reached over and flipped the red switch. From somewhere came a low hum, followed by a screeching metallic noise.

"Nancy!" George cried, grabbing her shoulder. "The side of the cage—it's moving this way! It's going to crush us!"

"'Bye, girls," Patrick said from the doorway. "Have a nice day!"

Even after the door slammed shut, they could hear his laughter echoing in the passage.

Chapter

Fifteen

Nancy and George could only stare at the slowly approaching wall of steel bars.

"This is just like what happened to Amelia at the end of *The Deadly Chamber!*" George said, her fear obvious in the shakiness of her voice.

"How did Amelia escape?" Nancy asked. "Maybe it'll work for us, too."

George shook her head. "Roderick Moore, the dashing highwayman who was reformed by his love for her, came to her rescue. I don't think we can count on anything like that."

"Come on, we've got to try to stop it," Nancy said. She planted her feet firmly, grabbed two bars of the moving wall, and shoved with all her strength. Next to her, George did the same.

It took only a few seconds to realize they were

wasting their energy. The wall had already moved over a foot toward them, leaving only about eight feet of cage for the girls.

"We've got to do something!" George said urgently. "What if we pushed something down into the track the wall is riding in? What's in your shoulder bag?"

Nancy quickly retrieved it from the floor. "Your cassette player and the flashlight from our room," she replied.

"Could we wedge the flashlight between the bars somehow?"

"Great idea!" Nancy exclaimed. She thrust the flashlight into the gap between two bars on the long side of the cage, just an inch from the moving wall. She held it in place until the steel frame of the moving wall met it. Then she stepped back, holding her breath.

A moment later the wall rolled right over the flashlight, crushing it. With a clatter, the flashlight fell to the floor.

"Nancy, it's hopeless!" George exclaimed. "There's no way we can stop that wall!"

Nancy's eyes moved frantically around the room. "Wait, I have an idea," she announced.

She grabbed the ruined flashlight, detached the headphones from George's tape player, and tied the thin headphone cord tightly around the flashlight. Thrusting her arm through the bars as far as she could reach, she set the flashlight swinging like a pendulum. It flew out in wider and wider arcs as Nancy aimed it at the red switch on the opposite wall, some five feet away.

"You almost got it!" George said, encouraging her.

Nancy strained, reaching her arm out as far as she could, but it was useless. At her farthest reach, she was still six inches short of hitting the switch.

"I'm sorry, George," she said dejectedly, reeling in the cord.

George glanced at the approaching wall, which was now about four feet from them. "How much longer do you think . . . ?"

"Five minutes, at the most," Nancy replied, studying the wall's progress. "The one thing I'm glad about is that we got Patrick's confession on tape. The police will find it when they find us. He won't get away with his crimes."

"I'm glad to hear that," George said dryly. "But I'd rather be around to see it."

"Me, too. But—" Nancy tossed the wrecked flashlight up and down in her hand. Suddenly her body stiffened. "Cross your fingers, George!" she exclaimed. "We haven't run out of hope yet!"

Once more she unwound the cord from around the flashlight, thrust it through the bars, and started swinging it. This time, she didn't aim it at the switch on the wall. Instead, she angled it toward the folding chair that Patrick had knocked over.

"If I can just snare the chair and pull it within reach, I might be able to throw it at the switch to turn it off," she explained.

George was dubious, but said nothing while Nancy swung the flashlight.

Sweat beaded on Nancy's brow as she swung the flashlight, trying to hook it around the top of the chair. Twice, the flashlight hit the chair and bounced off. The third time, it missed altogether.

"Hurry, Nancy," George said, clutching the bars next to Nancy. "Hurry!"

Nancy didn't need to be told. The moving wall was already beginning to nudge her shoulder. She reeled in the cord and swung the flashlight again, giving it an extra flick of the wrist. The flashlight soared upward, stopped with a jerk in midair as it reached the end of the cord, and fell straight down on the far side of the chair's back leg. Nancy let out her breath with a loud whoosh.

Slowly and steadily she pulled on the cord, so that the flashlight snagged on the chair leg. Then she pulled it across the floor toward them. Finally it was close enough for her to grab.

"Yes!" Nancy crowed. She grabbed a leg in each hand and stood up, lifting the chair until the back almost touched the ceiling. Then she swung it in a downward arc, aiming at the power switch.

There was a loud crash, and then silence. The scraping noise of the advancing bars had stopped.

"Nancy, you did it!" George shouted. She squeezed around the now narrow cage to give Nancy a big hug.

Nancy's whole body sagged with relief. She opened her clenched fists and let the folding chair crash to the floor.

"That was close," she said. "Much too close."

"But you did it!" George repeated. "You were terrific!"

"Thanks," Nancy said, her mind already racing ahead. "I don't see any obvious way out of this cage, do you?"

"What about picking the lock?"

"I don't think so," Nancy said. "I didn't bring my lock picking set with me, and we don't have anything else to use."

"This is ridiculous!" George said, hitting the bars in frustration. "There *must* be a way out of here."

"Know any reformed highwaymen named Roderick?" Nancy asked, raising an eyebrow. Then she began to study the wall that had been moving. "Look at this," she said with a puzzled frown. "The uprights at each end go down into those slits that run the length of the cage. There must be a motor under the floor that pushes the wall along."

George peered down at the narrow slits. "So?"

Nancy craned her neck and looked up. "At the top, the two uprights ride in tracks that keep them in place," she continued. "The setup is kind of like the sliding glass doors people have in their homes, except that the wall moves back and forth instead of sideways."

"Are you saying we could somehow move it back and get out that way?" George asked.

"I don't think so," Nancy replied. "But I watched some repair people put new glass in our neighbor's sliding door once. I thought they'd have to take the frame apart, to get the door out. But they just lifted it, until the bottom cleared the edge of the frame. Then all they had to do was tilt the door out. There was extra space in the top part of the framework—it was designed that way."

"I get it," George said. "Now that you mention it, the sliding glass doors on my stereo cabinet work that way, too." She eyed the wall of steel bars. "Do you think—"

"Maybe," Nancy replied. "The crosspiece at the top is a few inches lower than the ceiling. And the people who built this contraption must have had *some* way to install the moving wall. Come on, let's give it a try."

She bent her knees and got a good grip on two of the bars. Next to her, George did the same. "Ready?" Nancy said. "One—two—*heave!*"

Every muscle in her arms, legs, and back felt as if it were going to burst. She shut her eyes and clenched her jaw, summoning every ounce of energy she had.

At first the wall didn't budge. Then, she felt a movement so slight that she was afraid she was imagining it. No, it was real! The two prongs that supported it were slowly emerging from the narrow slits in the floor.

"Nancy, look out!"

Nancy and George pressed themselves against the opposite wall of the cage as the steel framework began to tilt, then to fall. It crashed to the floor with a din that shook the entire room. They were free!

There wasn't a second to lose. Grabbing her shoulder bag, Nancy checked to make sure that the cassette that held Patrick's confession was secure.

"Come on. We'd better warn the others about Patrick!"

The two girls hurried through the tunnels until Nancy managed to recognize the side passage that led to the small file room off Dorothea's study. She activated the latch and pushed the bookcase door open.

"What?" Kate exclaimed, springing up from the desk. The fear faded from her face as she recognized Nancy and George.

"Call Lieutenant Kitridge," Nancy blurted

out. "Patrick's the one who killed Maxine. He just tried to kill us, too."

For an instant Kate was unable to move as she took in the meaning of what Nancy had said. Finally she grabbed the telephone and punched in the emergency number. She handed the receiver to Nancy.

"We'll be right over," the lieutenant said, when Nancy finished telling him what she'd discovered about Patrick. "Stay where you are and don't take any chances. This is what the police are trained to do."

Nancy hung up and turned to Kate, who had listened in silent shock to Nancy's telephone conversation. "Do you have any idea where Patrick is now?" Nancy asked.

"He was here just a few minutes ago, to get the key to the display room. He's been doing an inventory of Dorothea's collection." Kate turned pale. "Nancy, we've got to stop him! There are enough weapons in there to start a war!"

Nancy spun and ran out of the room. At the doorway, she barreled into Julian, who grabbed her and kept her from sprawling. Two words of explanation, and he was dashing down the hall with her in the direction of the display room. Nancy could hear George and Kate close behind.

As she rounded a corner, Nancy saw that the door to the display room was open. She glimpsed Patrick inside, next to a display of antique pistols. He had a pad in one hand and a pen in the other. As the group charged to the doorway, he spun around to face them. His eyes widened in disbelief when he saw Nancy and George.

"What!" he shouted, rage making his body twitch. Dropping the pen, he grabbed a pistol from the display and aimed it at Nancy.

Nancy gasped and flung herself to one side as Patrick squeezed the trigger.

The only result was a loud click. Patrick then threw the pistol at Julian, who dodged before launching himself into a flying tackle that brought Patrick down. A moment later Patrick was facedown on the floor, with Julian's knee on his back.

Outside, blaring sirens drew nearer and nearer, then fell silent.

"What do you think you're doing?" Patrick demanded, twisting his head to Nancy. "I haven't done anything. You can't prove a thing!"

Nancy held up George's tape recorder. "It's all here," she told him. "In your own words and your own voice."

Patrick gave a convulsive twist but couldn't escape Julian's grip.

Half a dozen police officers came running into the display room with Lieutenant Kitridge in the lead. While his officers handcuffed Patrick, the lieutenant surveyed the scene.

"Great work," he told Nancy. "Where this

guy's going, he won't ever be able to hurt anyone again."

"Even though we've been through so much, it's kind of sad to be leaving Mystery Mansion," George said later Sunday afternoon.

She, Nancy, Kate, Julian, Vanessa, and Professor Coining had gotten together in the living room once again, this time to hear the story of Patrick's arrest. Their bags were packed and standing in the front hall. After a farewell toast, they would all be going their separate ways.

"I know what you mean," Nancy said. "I'm going to miss everyone, too."

Kate came over with a tray of cups of cider, and handed one each to Nancy and George. "I just found out that we won't be able to reschedule the conference for a while," she said. "The foundation has decided to hold off opening the museum until we find out the full extent of Patrick's crimes."

"What a shame," Professor Coining put in. "He seemed like such an intelligent, charming young man."

"It just goes to show, appearances can be deceiving," Julian said, putting his arm around Kate. Nancy guessed they had decided to give their romance a shot after all.

Leaning close to George, Nancy whispered, "I'm really happy for—"

She broke off as a voice behind her said, "Excuse me, Nancy."

Nancy looked around to see Erika standing in the doorway, next to Sergeant Wilensky.

"Erika! You're free!" Kate exclaimed, hurrying over to her.

"Thanks to Nancy and George," Erika said, smiling at the two girls. Grabbing Kate's hands, she said, "Kate, we've got to talk. With Patrick's arrest, *The Crooked Heart* is hot, hot, hot. And now that Maxine's gone, I'm the only editor in the business who really knows and understands Dorothea's work."

Nancy rolled her eyes at George. The old Erika was definitely back!

While Erika buttonholed Kate, Vanessa walked up to Nancy and said, "Perhaps *you* should think about writing a mystery novel."

"Thanks, but I'm a detective, not a writer," Nancy said, blushing.

"Well, think about it," Vanessa added. "You've got the experience to write a guaranteed bestseller!"

Nancy's next case:

Nancy and Bess have been offered the chance of a lifetime: a behind-the-scenes look at Mitchell's department store's star-studded Thanksgiving Day parade. But this year's gala event is following a perilous route. Someone is determined to flatten the floats, burst the balloons, and sabotage the entire spectacle—no matter who gets hurt.

The Thanksgiving feast of felonies leaves a sour taste in Nancy's mouth. She's learned that the police already have a prime suspect—Bess—and they have evidence to back up their charge. Nancy knows she'll have to work fast: Not only could the parade be headed for disaster, but her best friend could be headed for jail . . . in *DANGER ON PARADE,* Case #77 in the Nancy Drew Files™.